镜子书 · 新编经典童话绘本系列

团结篇

THE WIZARD OF OZ

绿野仙踪

[意]曼纽拉·阿德雷亚尼 绘

[美]弗兰克·鲍姆 著

李静滢 译

SPM 南方传媒 广东人民出版社
· 广州 ·

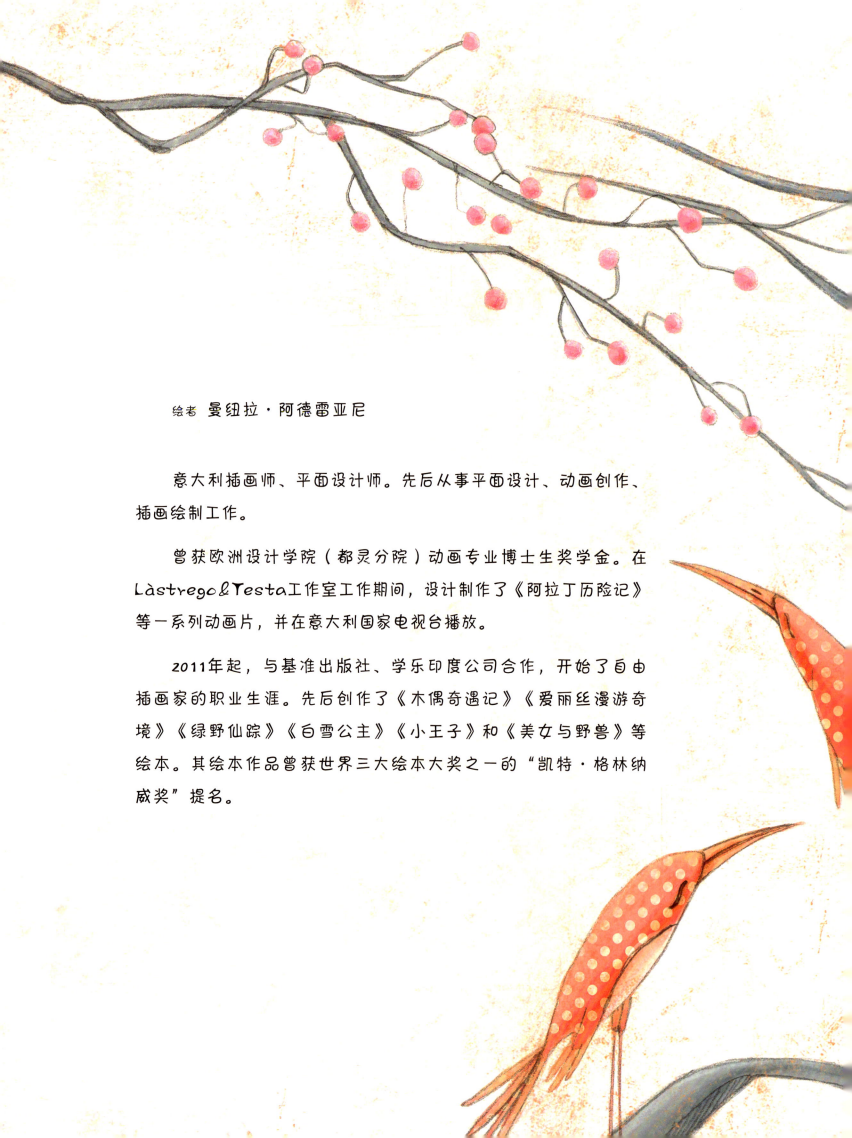

绘者 **曼纽拉·阿德雷亚尼**

意大利插画师、平面设计师。先后从事平面设计、动画创作、插画绘制工作。

曾获欧洲设计学院（都灵分院）动画专业博士生奖学金。在Làstrego&Testa工作室工作期间，设计制作了《阿拉丁历险记》等一系列动画片，并在意大利国家电视台播放。

2011年起，与基准出版社、学乐印度公司合作，开始了自由插画家的职业生涯。先后创作了《木偶奇遇记》《爱丽丝漫游奇境》《绿野仙踪》《白雪公主》《小王子》和《美女与野兽》等绘本。其绘本作品曾获世界三大绘本大奖之一的"凯特·格林纳威奖"提名。

做个团结朋友的孩子

你折断过树枝吗？一根小树枝很容易折断，但是十根小树枝放在一起却很难被折断。这就是团结创造的魔法。

多萝茜本来只是一个普通的小女孩，可是在遇到稻草人、铁皮人和胆小的狮子以后，在他们的帮助下，她完成了一个又一个不可能的冒险。这就是团结创造的魔法。

你愿意做个团结朋友的孩子，感受它的魔法吗？

有个小女孩，名字叫多萝茜。

她最好的朋友是一只名叫托托的小狗。多萝茜和她的叔叔婶婶一起生活。他们住的房子是灰蒙蒙的，周围的平原是灰蒙蒙的，他们的心情也总是灰蒙蒙的，但是小狗托托给她的生活带来了亮色，带来了欢乐。托托的毛不是灰色的，它有一身棕色和白色相间的漂亮皮毛。托托的尾巴总是摇个不停。它总是用一双滴溜溜的黑眼睛盯着多萝茜，缠着她逗它玩耍。

不过今天多萝茜没心思陪托托玩。她惴惴不安，担心就要发生不同寻常的事了，因为她看到亨利叔叔不安地望着天空，而天空比平时阴暗得多。远处传来了呼啸的风声。风越来越大，草随风起伏，仿佛掀起了波浪。亨利叔叔突然跳起来。"爱姆，龙卷风来了！"他朝妻子喊道，"赶紧下地窖！"

托托被亨利叔叔的叫喊声吓坏了。它从多萝茜的臂弯里蹿出来，钻到了床底下。多萝茜连忙追过去捉它。爱姆婶婶正在洗碟子，她只朝门外瞥了一眼，就知道他们的处境是多么危险了。她赶紧扔下碟子，拔腿奔到屋子中央，打开地板上的活动门，顺着梯子往地窖里爬，同时对多萝茜大喊道："过来，多萝茜，快过来！"

多萝茜终于捉住了托托，跟着婶婶往地窖那边跑，但她刚跑到半路，意外就发生了。呼啸的风声突然变得震耳欲聋，房子剧烈地晃动起来，多萝茜再也站不稳，一下子坐到地板上。她感到房子旋转了两圈，然后飘了起来，越飘越高，一直飘到了龙卷风的最顶端。

她向窗外看了看，看到房子旁边飘着亨利叔叔家的牛和马，他还没来得及把它们赶回马厩。托托可不喜欢这样在空中摇荡。它在房间里来回跑动，大声狂吠，跑得太靠近地板上打开的活动门，结果掉了出去。多萝茜吓坏了，以为再也见不到它了，但是过了一会儿，她看见活动门那里露出了托托的鼻子。风太大了，强风托住了它，所以它没摔下去。多萝茜连忙爬到门口，把小狗拉进屋子里，用力关上了活动门。她抱着托托坐在地板上，一动不动地听着周围的风声。

　　时间显得如此漫长，这一切仿佛永远也不会结束。她不知道房子会不会掉到地面摔个粉碎，会不会被风撕成碎片，但是目前还没发生什么可怕的事，所以她慢慢平静下来，等着看会发生什么。最后她从地板爬到床上，紧紧抱着托托，闭上眼睛睡着了。房子就像一片轻盈的羽毛，在空中飘荡了一整夜。

　　多萝茜是被一声巨响和剧烈的震动惊醒的。她吓得闭紧了双眼，直到托托舔她

的手才睁开眼睛，她知道小狗比她更害怕。她坐起来，看到房子不再旋转，风已经停了，黑夜已经过去，明亮的阳光透过窗户照进来，洒满了房间。

多萝茜跳下床，跑到门口打开房门，向四周看了一下，不禁发出一声惊奇的叫喊。她看见的景象太奇异了。

旋风把房子带到了一个绝美的地方。这里到处盛开着鲜艳的花朵，不远处有一条小溪，水声淙淙，色彩斑斓的小鸟在水边梳洗着漂亮的羽毛。多萝茜看见一小群人沿着小路走过来，边走边朝她高声呼唤。他们有三男一女，是小女孩多萝茜见过的最奇怪的人。他们戴着高高的蓝色锥形帽子，帽子上挂着铃铛，每走一步铃铛都轻快地叮当作响。三个男人的衣服是蓝色的，长长的胡须和尖尖的鞋子也是蓝色的。但是那小个子女人穿着一件白色的长袍，上面装饰着钻石一样闪闪发亮的星星。快走到小屋时，三个男人停住了，在那里踟蹰不前，好像有些害怕。

小个子女人走上来，朝多萝茜深深地鞠了一躬，说道："最强大的女巫啊，欢迎来到芒奇金人的土地！你杀死了东方的邪恶女巫，把人们从奴役中解放出来，我们不知道怎样感谢你才好。"

多萝茜吃惊得说不出话来。这小个子女人称她为"女巫"，还说她杀死了东方的邪恶女巫，这究竟是什么意思呢？她从未伤害过别人，他们肯定是认错人了！她必须纠正他们的错误，所以她迟疑着说道："谢谢你的好意，但你肯定弄错了，我从来都没杀过人！"

"但你的房子确实这样做了！"小个子女人指着房子一角回答。

那里露出了两只脚，脚上套着一双华丽的红靴子。

"天啊！不！我做了什么？怎么会这样啊？真的太抱歉了，我想不到会这样，我们要做点什么吗？"

"没什么需要做的。"小个子女人微笑着回答。

"可是，她是谁呢？"多萝茜问。

"她正是东方的邪恶女巫，"小个子女人回答，"许多年来，她一直奴役生活在这个地方的芒奇金人。现在芒奇金人终于自由了，他们想感谢你的恩惠。"

"你是芒奇金人吗？"多萝茜问。她仍然感到十分困惑。

小个子女人回答道："不是，但我是他们的朋友。芒奇金人找我过来，我立刻就来了。我居住在北方的大地上，我是北方女巫。"

"女巫？你真的是个女巫？"

"是真的，不过我是善良女巫，每个人都爱我。我并不是唯一的女巫，奥兹国有四个女巫，其中住在北方和南方的两个是善良女巫。这是真的，因为我自己就是其中一个。但是住在东方和西方的两个是邪恶女巫。现在你已经把她们中的一个杀死了，奥兹国只剩下一个邪恶女巫，就是住在西方的那

个。奥兹自己也是巫师，他是个男巫师。"小个子女人说。

"男巫师？还有男巫师？"多萝茜吃惊地问，"刚才你说他叫什么名字来着？"

"我的孩子，他的名字叫奥兹，他是个法力十分强大的男巫师，住在翡翠城。"她还想继续往下说，这时，一直沉默地站在旁边的芒奇金人突然惊叫起来。他们指着屋子的一角，邪恶女巫的脚露出来的地方。"什么事？"北方女巫问，接着又说，"哦，东方邪恶女巫太老了，在太阳光下很快就被晒干了。除了一双红靴子，她什么也没留下来。小姑娘，这双靴子现在属于你了，你拿着吧。"

一个芒奇金人跑上去拾起那双靴子，拂去了灰尘，把它交给多萝茜。"东方女巫很珍惜这双靴子，"他说，"它们肯定具有魔力，虽然我们不知道是什么魔力。"多萝茜接过靴子，说了声谢谢。她脱下自己灰色的旧木头鞋，换上了这双漂亮靴子，然后问道："我很想回家，我的叔叔婶婶肯定在担心我。你们能帮我找到回家的路吗？"

"很抱歉，"北方女巫说，"我不知道你回家的路该怎么走。在东方，有无边无际的大沙漠，没有人能穿越那片沙漠。在北方，也是无边无际的沙漠。北方我了解，那里是我的家。"

"在南方同样是大沙漠，"一个芒奇金人说，"据说在西方也是一样。整个奥兹国的周围都围绕着大沙漠！"

"我想，你将不得不和我们生活在一起了。"北方女巫总结道。听到这句话，多萝茜开始啜泣。小狗托托凑到她身旁小声叫着，但是它也无法安慰多萝茜。"啊，亲爱的，别哭了，或许我们能找到办法！"小个子的北方女巫说，"这很简单，但要经过非常艰难、极其危险的旅程。"

"我需要怎么做？"多萝茜擦干眼泪问道。

"到翡翠城去。也许奥兹能帮助你，只有他的力量足够强大，应该有能力帮你回家。"

"翡翠城在哪里？"多萝茜问道。

"在这片土地的中心。去翡翠城的路全部是用黄砖铺设的，只要沿着黄砖铺的路走，你就不会迷路。路程很长，你会路过美丽的地方，也会路过可怕、恐怖的地方。"北方女巫说。

"你能和我一起去吗？"多萝茜满怀希望地问。

"我不能去翡翠城，但我会留给你一个吻，那样在这里就没人敢伤害你了。"说完，她走到多萝茜身边，温柔地吻了吻多萝茜的前额。她亲吻过的地方立刻放出了光芒。女巫说："你到了翡翠城，就把你的故事告诉奥兹。我相信他能帮你。我的孩子，再会了。"女巫原地旋转了三圈，随即消失不见了。

三个芒奇金人向多萝茜鞠躬道别，然后离开了。

"好啦，托托，现在只剩下我们两个了。你害怕吗？反正我是有点儿害怕。不过我们必须勇敢，要去找用黄砖铺设的路，沿着那条路走到翡翠城。只有到了那里，我们才能找到回家的办法。你做好出发的准备了吗？"小狗托托用黑溜溜的眼睛盯着她，摇着尾巴，表示什么都明白了。多萝茜回到房子里，找到一个篮子，又从橱柜里拿了些面包。然后她关好房门，系好靴子的鞋带，和托托一起出发了。

明亮的太阳高挂在空中，许多小鸟在枝头歌唱，托托汪汪叫着追赶那些小鸟。多萝茜看着托托，微笑起来，很快她就发现自己不再害怕了。

多萝茜也不再觉得孤独。每个芒奇金人都知道是她把他们从邪

恶女巫的奴役中解放出来的，那些身穿蓝色衣服的矮个子只要看到她走过来，都会放下手里的农活，跑来向她鞠躬。每一次她都会微笑着回应他们的问候，托托转着圈跳来跳去，开心地汪汪叫，这让那些芒奇金人十分惊奇，因为他们以前从没见过狗。

走了一个多小时后，多萝茜决定停下来休息。她爬到路边的篱笆墙上坐下来。墙那边是一块玉米地，她看见一个用来吓唬鸟的稻草人被绑在玉米地正中央立着的木头杆子顶端。多萝茜从篮子里拿出面包，给了托托一块，然后边吃面包边凝视着稻草人。这个稻草人让她觉得有点奇怪，却又说不出哪里奇怪。乍看上去，他就是个非常普通的稻草人，穿着旧衣服、旧鞋子，他的头是个小布口袋，里面塞满了稻草，上面画着眼睛、鼻子和嘴巴。多萝茜正认真地观察稻草人那张画出来的脸，却看见稻草人向她眨着眼睛，不禁大吃一惊。"托托，我肯定是看花眼了！可是……"话没说完，稻草人就朝她微微点了点头。这下不用怀疑了，稻草人是在叫她过去！多萝茜怯生生地从篱笆墙上溜下来，走进了玉米地。

"你好。"稻草人清了清嗓子，和多萝茜打了个招呼。

"你在讲话吗？你真的在讲话吗？"多萝茜无比惊讶地问。

"当然，"稻草人回答说，"你能和我聊聊天吗？你好吗？"

"我……我很好，只是听到你会说话，有点吃惊，这也太……"多萝茜想了想，又很有礼貌地补充了一句，"你好吗？"

"我不太好，感觉非常烦。我整天整夜被吊在这里吓跑乌鸦，已经好几个星期了，我背上插着木杆，太难受了。你能放我下来吗？"多萝茜走上前，伸手把稻草人从木杆上取了下来。她没费什么力气，因为稻草人身体里塞的是稻草，没有多少重量。"多谢你！"说完，稻草人开始舒展肢体，伸懒腰，弯腰，左右扭动。

"感觉好多了，真的好多了！"做完了他独特的舒展动作后，稻草人说，"我真不知道该怎么感谢你，我连你的名字都还不知道呢。你是谁呀？"

"我的名字叫多萝茜，我的家在堪萨斯州……那说来话长。我要去翡翠城找伟大的奥兹，请他帮我回家。"

"奥兹是谁？"稻草人好奇地问。

"什么，你不知道吗？"多萝茜吃惊地说。

"不知道，我什么也不知道。我是用稻草填满的，所以我没脑子。"稻草人难过地摇了摇头，悲伤地回答。

"我真的很抱歉！"多萝茜说。

稻草人又问："如果我和你一起去翡翠城，奥兹会不会给我头脑？"

"我不知道，"多萝茜回答道，"如果你愿意，可以和我一起去。值得一试，你觉得呢？"

"这倒是真的，"稻草人说，"你看，我的躯干、双腿和手臂是用稻草填塞的，这些我都不在乎，因为这样我就不会觉得痛，就不会受伤了，哪怕有人打我，或者拿针刺我……但是我真的非常想有头脑。当一个蠢货，真的实在太糟糕了！"

他的真诚触动了多萝茜。"你绝对应该跟我和托托一起去。"她坚决地说。

"谢谢你！"稻草人感激地回答。多萝茜帮他翻过了篱笆墙，随后，他们沿着黄砖铺设的路出发了。

托托对稻草人的加入并不满意。它低沉地吠叫着，警觉地嗅着这个新同伴。"托托！别这样！"多萝茜斥责道，接着又对稻草人说，"不要害怕托托，它不会咬你的。""唔，我不怕，"稻草人开心地回答，"就算它咬到我，我也不怕，它不可能咬伤稻草！这世上只有一样东西让我怕得要死，就是一根点着的火柴！"他一边说，一边大踏步往前走。

这时他们已经沿着路走进了树林，但是没走几步，稻草人就踩进了坑里，脸朝下跌倒在黄砖铺设的路上。要知道这段路真是太难走了，到处都是树根，所以坑坑洼洼的。遇到有坑的地方，托托会跳过去，多萝茜会绕过去，但是稻草人没有脑子，只知道笔直地向前走，每走一步都磕磕绊绊。好在他怎么都不会摔伤。多萝茜把他拉起来，他们就这样继续往前走，一路走一路闲聊。"我真不明白，你为什么想离开这个美丽的地方，回到到处都灰蒙蒙的堪萨斯州呢？你能告诉我吗？"稻草人问道。多萝茜不想刺伤自己的朋友，但还是回答说："你不明白，是因为你没头脑，你要是有头脑就会明白，别的地方再好，也比不上自己的家。"

"这我还是第一次听说。不过我并不吃惊。我是几星期前才被人做出来的，也从来都没有家。我一直都在那片田地中间，和我聊天的只有乌鸦。记得有一天，我抱怨说插在背后的杆子很难受，一只乌鸦和我说，哪怕我有一丁点头脑，也早就离开这地方了。所以我明白了，在这个世界上，头脑是最重要的东西，我下决心要全力争取得到个头脑。我真想一步就迈到翡翠城！"稻草人正说着，却看到多萝茜坐到一棵树下，打起了哈欠。"你怎么啦？"他问道。"我累坏了，天也要黑了……我们能停下来睡一会儿吗？"多萝茜问道。托托蜷缩着依偎到她身边。"当然。等一下，我想到个办法。"稻草人说。他开始从衬衣里往外拽稻草，而后把草铺到地上。"弄

好啦！"他说，
"躺在稻草上，你就不会觉得冷
了。"多萝茜在稻草上躺下来，立刻就睡着了。
托托趴在她身边，永远不知疲倦的稻草人站在树下等着
天亮。

太阳升起时，托托睁开了眼睛，打了个哈欠，急切地舔着多萝茜的鼻
子，要把她叫醒。多萝茜醒了，站了起来，看见稻草人静静地在一旁等着
她。"早上好！我们能走了吗？"他问道。

"稍等一下，"她对他说，"我得先去找点水。"

稻草人问："你要水干吗？"

"洗脸，还要喝。"

"这样看来，有个肉做的身体肯定很麻烦！你必须喝水、洗脸、睡觉。
但是不管怎么样，你有头脑，只要能思考，再麻烦也都值得。"稻草人坚

定地点了点头，得出了他的结论。接着他把稻草塞回去，和多萝茜一起离开黄砖铺设的路，跟在托托后面穿过树林。小狗似乎非常清楚能在哪里找到清水，他们很快就发现了一条清澈的小溪，多萝茜在溪边洗漱后喝了个痛快。他们正要回到那条黄砖路，却听见森林中传来了呻吟的声音。

多萝茜赶紧抓住开始狂吠的托托，问道："那是什么？"

"我猜不出，"稻草人回答说，"但我们可以过去看看。"这时他们身后又传来了一声呻吟。他们转过身，朝发出声音的地方走过去，走了几步，多萝茜就看到树丛中间有个亮闪闪的东西。多萝茜十分好奇地跑过去，可是没跑多远就突然停住了，因为她看到了那个亮闪闪的东西，或者说是亮闪闪的人。一棵大树旁有一个完全用铁皮做的人，他的手高举过头顶，手里紧握着一把斧头。他的头、手臂和腿脚都连接在他的身上，但他就那么一动不动地站在大树旁边，好像困在那里不能动弹。多萝茜绕着他走了一圈，非常惊奇地注视着他，这时稻草人也赶了过来，同样惊奇地注视着这个铁皮人。托托不停地大声狂吠着，一次次去咬铁皮人的腿，结果却只是伤到了自己的牙齿。"你好，"多萝茜问，"你能听见我说话吗？"

"我能，我能听见你说话。"铁皮人回答她。

"是你在呻吟吗？"

"是的，我已经呻吟了一年多，但是没有一个人听到我的呻吟，也没有一个人来救我。"

多萝茜被铁皮人那忧愁的声音触动了，说道："我们愿意帮你，但是我们能做什么呢？我们该怎么帮你？"

"啊，谢谢你！那边就是我的小屋，桌上有个油罐。把油罐拿过来，给我的各个关节上点油，求求你了，我生锈得太厉害了，一点也动不了。如果给我加了油，我就能获得新生了！"

多萝茜立刻跑到他说的小屋里，找到了油罐，然后跑回大树下。她跑得上气不接下气，着急地问道："我拿来了！哪些地方要加油？"

"先把油加到我的头颈上。"铁皮人回答。多萝茜赶紧往铁皮人的颈部倒了点儿油，但是那里锈得太厉害，稻草人只好捧着铁皮人的头，轻缓地左右摇晃了好多次，最后铁皮人的头终于能动了。"现在请把油加在我的手臂和腿的关节上吧。"他说。稻草人又小心地弯曲着铁皮人的手臂和腿，多萝茜不停地往关节上浇油，直到铁皮人能自由活动为止。"我真不知道该怎么感谢你们！"他鞠了一躬，说道，"这个地方不会有人路过，如果不是你们，我可能会永远困在这里。不过你们怎么会走到这树林里呢？"

"我们要到翡翠城去，拜访那伟大的奥兹巫师，"多萝茜回答，"我要请求他送我回到堪萨斯州，稻草人要请求他在他的脑袋里放进个脑子。"铁皮人沉默了片刻，随后问道："你觉得奥兹能给我一颗心吗？""我不知道。但是应该可以吧！"看到铁皮人又要哭了，多萝茜赶紧说道，"如果他能给稻草人一个脑子，应该也能给你一颗心。""那我想和你们一起去，"铁皮人说完又对稻草人说，"你想有头脑吗？从前我是有头脑的，但我现在想要的已经不是头脑了。我和你说的是真话，如果要我在头脑和心之间选择，那我绝对会选择一颗心。

"我告诉你，心是这世界上最重要的东西！"

铁皮人笃定地说。稻草人问："为什么呢？""我把我的故事告诉你，你就明白了。"他们穿过树林时，铁皮人讲了他的故事："我生来并不是铁皮人，而是个普通的樵夫。有一天我遇到了一个女孩子，她是芒奇金人。我爱上了她，做梦都想娶她，所以我加倍努力地工作，想建一栋大房子和她一起住。但是，那个女孩子在东方邪恶女巫的宫殿里工作，女巫不想放她走，于是在我砍树的斧头上施了巫术。我干活时，斧头突然从我手里滑了出去，砍掉了我的一条腿。你能想象到我是多么绝望吧？但是村里的铁皮匠想了个办法，给我装了一条铁皮做的新腿，于是我就又回去工作了。但是在那之后，斧头又从我手里滑出去，砍掉了我的另一条腿，后来斧头又砍掉了我的双臂。铁皮匠再次救了我，用铁皮给我做了新的手臂和腿，安到了身体上。我又回到林中砍树，最后被邪恶女巫施了巫术的斧头砍掉了我的头，那一瞬间我想，我真的完蛋了。但是铁皮匠又救了我，替我装了个包着铁皮的新头。我以为我打败了那个邪恶女巫。直到有一天，斧头砍在了我的胸口。我跑到铁皮匠那里，他给我换了个铁皮做的身体，但是他无法给我安一颗心。我再也感受不到对芒奇金女子的爱，也没有娶她的想法了。

"再也没有什么能伤到我。我就这样自给自足地生活了很多年，直到有一天，我遇到了一场暴风雨，大雨淋得我浑身湿透，接着我的关节就生了锈。我一动不动地在树林里站了一年。受困这么久，真是件可怕的事情，但也让我有了时间思考。我意识到，我在恋爱时是幸福的，是世界上最快乐的人，然而一个没有心的人无法去爱。我终于明白了，我最大的损失就是失去了我的心。所以现在我要去请求奥兹给我一颗心。如果他能给我一颗心，我会回去找那个芒奇金女孩，如果她还单身，我想请求她嫁给我。"

多萝茜和稻草人认真地听完了铁皮人的故事，突然发现黄砖路越来越窄，树木越来越浓密，天色越来越阴暗。密林中不时传来奇特的吼叫声，怪异的声音让小女孩多萝茜的心越来越慌。托托也害怕了，它紧贴在多萝茜身旁，不敢再跑开半步。

突然间，森林中传来了可怕的吼声。接着，一只大狮子猛地一跃，跳到

了路当中。它爪子一挥，把稻草人打倒在路边，随后又伸爪子去抓铁皮人，但是狮子无法抓伤铁皮人，这让它大吃一惊，愤怒之下转身要攻击多萝茜，小狗托托看到小主人有危险，立刻冲上前拼命向狮子吠叫。这只猛兽张开嘴要咬小狗，但多萝茜不顾危险冲向前，尽全力猛掴它的鼻子，同时高声喊起来："你怎么敢咬托托！你应该为自己感到惭愧，你这么大的家伙还要咬一只小狗！""可我没咬到它。"狮子说话时揉着自己的鼻子，那正是被多萝茜打中的地方。"没咬到，但你想咬它，"多萝茜反驳说，"你就是个胆小鬼！""是的，我知道，我是个胆小鬼，"狮子回答，"我一直知道自己是个胆小鬼，但我能怎么办呢？""首先，你不应该去打可怜的稻草人，他只是个填塞着稻草的人！"多萝茜气哼哼地说。"他是用稻草填塞的吗？所以我没有伤到他！那个人是金属做的吗？"狮子又指着铁皮人说，"所以我的脚爪才无法抓伤他啊！呃，这只是什么东西，它是用铁皮做的还是用稻草填塞的？"女孩子说："都不是。它是小动物，是我的小狗。""啊！现在我看清楚它了，它好小啊！谁都不会想伤害这么个小东西，除非像我这样的胆小鬼。"狮子摇了摇身上的鬃毛，愁容满面地说。

狮子看上去那么伤心，多萝茜都不忍心再责备它了。

"或许你可以不再当个胆小鬼。"多萝茜说。"可我不知道该怎么做，我生下来就是这样，"狮子回答说，"树林中所有的野兽都以为我很勇敢，因为狮子被称为万兽之王。于是我学会了把声音吼得非常响，让所有的动物都害怕，但是如果狗熊、老虎或大象想要向我挑战，我自己就会逃走了。我没办法，什么都会让我害怕！"狮子边说边用尾巴尖擦去一滴眼泪，"我一听到前面有危险，心就会狂跳！"

铁皮人说："这证明你有一颗心。你很幸运，因为我再也没有心了。"

"而我没有头脑。"稻草人插了一句。

"而我想回家。所以我们要去翡翠城，我们要去找奥兹巫师，请他给稻

草人头脑，给铁皮人一颗心，把我和托托送回堪萨斯州。"多萝茜总结道。

"如果你们不反对，我想和你们一起去，"狮子说，"我想去和巫师说，请他赐给我勇气。如果我一直是个胆小鬼，我一生都不会快乐的。"于是几个朋友又动身了，狮子威严地走在多萝茜身边。

这天他们走了不到一个小时，就看见路上横着一条沟壑，那沟壑又宽又深，侧壁十分陡峭，沟底参差不齐、犬牙差互。极目望去，只见沟壑把森林分成了两半。他们能看到沟壑对面的黄砖路，但是怎么才能过去呢？多萝茜焦急地问道："我们要怎么办啊？"狮子谨慎地估量了沟壑的宽度，说道："我想我能跳过去。""那太棒了！你可以背着我们跳过去，一次背一个，"稻草人说，"我第一个，因为我是稻草做的，就算摔下去也不会受伤。"狮子回答道："千万别提摔下去，别吓唬我，我自己已经很害怕了。好吧，你骑到我背上来吧！"稻草人爬到狮子背上，双手紧紧抓住了狮子的鬃毛。狮子在深沟旁边蹲了下来，接着用力一跃，跨过了深沟，平安地落到了另一边。"轻轻松松，"狮子高兴地说，接着又跳了回来，"谁第二个过？""我！"多萝茜抱起托托，说道。狮子起跳的那一瞬间，她似乎飞了起来，还没等她害怕，就已经平安地落到那一边了。狮子又回去把铁皮人背了过来。他们一起坐下，让狮子休息一会儿。来回的几次跳跃把它累坏了，它伸着舌头，气喘吁吁，好半天才歇过来。

沟壑这一边的森林十分浓密阴暗。狮子休息好了以后他们重新上路，但是走得很慢，时常要停下来，等铁皮人砍掉阻碍他们前进的树枝。他们走了好久好久，也没走出多远。走着走着，他们又遇到了一条深深的沟壑。这条沟壑太宽了，狮子立刻就意识到它跳不过去。

"如果沟再窄一些，我就能背着你们跳过去了，但是这条沟太宽了，我觉得我跳不过去！"狮子说，"这么宽，我一想就会怕得发抖。"

"我想到了个办法，"稻草人突然说，"你们看沟边那棵树，它好高大

啊！如果铁皮人能砍倒它，让它朝沟壑对面倒下去，就能搭起一座桥了。”

　　“这个想法太棒了，”铁皮人称赞道，“你可以相信，你脑袋里不仅塞满了稻草，稻草下面还是有脑子的！我要开工了。”

　　“赶快动手吧，”狮子小声说，“这片森林里有‘开力大’。”

　　“‘开力大’是什么？”多萝茜问。

　　狮子回答说：“它们是奇怪的野兽，身体像熊，头像老虎，脚爪长长的，让我心惊胆战。”

　　铁皮人立刻动手，仔细衡量后猛地劈了几斧头，那棵树很快就要倒了，

于是狮子用前腿抵住了树干，尽力往深沟那边推。大树终于倒了下去，树梢落到了沟的那一边。"好啦，我们走吧！"他们正要走上这座桥，却听见身后的树林里传来一声尖锐的咆哮。他们急忙转过身，只见两头巨大的野兽冲了过来，它们的头像老虎，身体像熊。

"'开力大'！"狮子哆嗦着叫道。

"快！"稻草人高声喊道，"快过桥！"

多萝茜臂弯里抱着托托朝前跑，稻草人和铁皮人跟在后面，狮子殿后。狮子虽然吓得发抖，但是为了让伙伴们安全离开，还是挺身而出面对'开力大'，闭上眼睛发出一声狂吼。那吼声震耳欲聋，惊得多萝茜和稻草人失声尖叫，就连'开力大'也停住了。但是'开力大'很快就发现自己体形比狮子大，而且狮子无法以一敌二，于是又冲了上来，毫不停留地跳上树干追赶他们。

"快跑！"狮子喊道，"我们要完蛋了，它们肯定会将我们撕成碎片。快跑，多萝茜，躲到我后面。"

稻草人喊道："别急！我有办法！铁皮人，快砍掉沟这边的树干！"

铁皮人立刻挥起斧头，就在两只'开力大'马上要扑过来时，两斧头砍断了树干。大树搭起的桥断了，连同两头猛兽一起落进了深沟。每个人都长舒了一口气。

狮子说道："这些猛兽真的把我吓坏了，我的心现在仍然怦怦乱跳。"

"唉，"铁皮人喃喃地说，"我倒宁愿有一颗会被惊吓到的心。"

经历了这次危险后，他们继续赶路时急切地加快了脚步，一心想尽快走出森林。他们走得太快了，最后多萝茜有点儿跟不上，只好骑到狮子背上让狮子驮着她走。好在走了几小时后，树木渐渐变得稀疏，他们终于走出了那

危机四伏的森林，来到一片漂亮的果园。他们十分欢欣地穿过了果园。走到下午时，道路突然断了，一条湍急的河流横在他们面前。在河的那一边，黄砖铺设的道路向前延伸，穿过一片美丽的草场，青葱的草地上点缀着五颜六色的花朵。"我们怎么才能过河，去那个美丽的地方呢？"多萝茜问。"这不难！"稻草人回答说，"铁皮人可以用树干造个木筏，我们就能乘木筏渡河了。"于是铁皮人又拿着斧头开始干活儿了。造木筏并不容易，天黑了，木筏还没造好，狮子、托托和多萝茜找了个安全的地方休息，铁皮人和稻草人继续造木筏。多萝茜睡着了，梦见了翡翠城，梦见了伟大的奥兹要立刻把她送回她在堪萨斯州的家。

第二天早晨，这个小团队的成员们精神饱满地准备出发。他们已经走出那片危机四伏的黑暗大森林，等待他们的是鲜花盛开的芳草地，只要他们过了河就可以漫步其间了。

木筏终于造好了，多萝茜坐在木筏中间，托托紧挨着她。狮子跨上这木筏时，木筏倾斜得很厉害，还好没有翻。稻草人和铁皮人各自撑着长木杆，把木筏向对岸划去。开始几分钟一切都很顺利，筏子慢慢朝对岸漂过去，但是到了河中间时，水变深了，长木杆很难触到河底。"啊，糟了，"铁皮人叫道，"我们如果无法校正航向，可能就会被水流带到西方邪恶女巫的领地，那我就永远得不到一颗心了。""我就得不到头脑了，"稻草人说，"我们必须到翡翠城。"说着，他十分用力地撑着长木杆，结果木杆插进了河底的淤泥，还没等他把木杆拔出来，木筏就被急流冲走了，稻草人只能抱住河中央的木杆悬在那里。"再见了，我的朋友！"木筏漂走时，他在后面喊道。铁皮人开始哭泣，却又立刻想起眼泪会让他生锈，于是赶紧忍住眼泪。每个人都很难过，很担心稻草人的命运。

稻草人此时想道："我的状况真的是毫无改进。之前我是后背插在竹竿上吊在玉米地里，那时我还可以和乌鸦聊聊天，可是立在河中木杆上的稻草人真的是毫无用处！"

木筏被流水冲着往下游漂去，过了一会儿，狮子说："我们必须自救！我想我能拖着木筏游到岸边，但是你们要紧紧拉住我的尾巴。"说完，狮子就深吸一口气，跳到水里，铁皮人用力紧紧抓着它的尾巴。狮子费尽力气，终于把木筏拖到了岸边。他们筋疲力尽地上了岸，坐了几分钟，思索着接下来该做什么。多萝茜做出了决定：

"我们必须回去帮稻草人上岸，然后再去找那条黄砖路。"

于是他们沿着河岸往上游走，去搜寻稻草人。当他们发现稻草人时，他仍然在河中间，抱着立在那里的木杆，愁容满面。他们在河岸坐下来，商量该怎么救稻草人，这时有一只鹳鸟飞过。鹳鸟看见了他们，停下来问道："你们是谁？你们要到哪里去？""我们要去翡翠城。"多萝茜回答。"不是这条路。你们迷路了吗？"鹳鸟问。"没有，我们知道必须回到黄砖路上，"多萝茜说，"但我们要先救朋友稻草人，他就在河中间。""我来试试看！"鹳鸟说。接着它朝抱着木杆的稻草人飞过去，在空中滑翔到稻草人上方，用强健的大爪子抓住稻草人，提着他飞回岸上。他的几个旅伴非常高兴地拥抱了他。"多谢你啊！"鹳鸟飞走前，他们由衷地对它表示感谢。

几个朋友劫后重逢，满心欢喜地继续上路。他们走进了一大片罂粟花田。"看啊，这些花多美啊！"多萝茜闻着馥郁的花香赞叹道。其实很多人都知道，罂粟花的香气太浓烈了，闻到的人很容易昏睡过去，而且一睡就再也醒不过来了，除非有人把他从罂粟花旁带走。但是小女孩多萝茜不知道这一点，她继续朝前走，遇到又大又漂亮的花朵时就会停下来闻一闻。很快她就感到眼皮越来越沉重，不由自主地停下脚步，闭上了眼睛。

铁皮人知道这个小女孩正处于危险之中。"我们必须立刻离开这片罂粟花田！稻草人，来帮帮我！"他们拉着多萝茜往前走，直到多萝茜再也坚持不住，迷迷糊糊睡着了。狮子问道："我们怎么办啊？如果我们把她留在这

里，她会死掉的！实际上，我觉得这些花的香气会让我们都死在这里，我也要睁不开眼睛了，托托已经睡着了。"但是铁皮人和稻草人一个身体是铁做的，一个身体是稻草做的，罂粟花香对他们没什么影响。稻草人回答："狮子，我们要做的就是——你赶快跑，能跑多快就跑多快。你太沉了，我们没那么大力量，不可能把你从花田里抬出去。我们会尽力救多萝茜和托托出去，但是你千万不能睡过去，你如果倒下去睡着了，我们真的不知道怎么帮你。"狮子听了这话，大步向前跳跃，跳了几下就不见了踪影。铁皮人和稻草人把手交叠起来当椅子，抬着多萝茜和托托往前走。他们走啊走啊，可这罂粟花田似乎无边无际，总也走不到头。他们沿着河岸前进，拐了个弯后看到了他们的狮子朋友，它躺在地上，已经昏睡过去，而前面不远处就是草地了。"天啊，可怜的朋友！"铁皮人难过地说。"我们帮不了他，"稻草人说，"它太重了，我们只能让它睡在这儿了。或许它会梦到自己成了最勇敢的动物吧。我们走吧，我们得把多萝茜抬到没有这种花的地方，不然等待她的也会是同样的命运。"

他们走到了没有罂粟花的草地上，多萝茜伸了伸胳膊，好像就要苏醒

过来了。稻草人和铁皮人把多萝茜放到柔软的草地上，又把小狗托托放在她身旁，等着新鲜的微风吹走罂粟花的最后一缕香气。稻草人说："我们差不多快走到被流水冲走的那个地方了，离那黄砖铺设的路肯定不远了，你说呢？"铁皮人正想回答，却听到一声吼叫，他转过头，看见一只奇异的野兽正在追赶一只田鼠。那野兽看起来有点像大野猫。铁皮人没有心，却仍然觉得，他不能坐视这样弱小无助的小田鼠被大猫杀死，于是他举起斧头吓唬那只大野猫。大猫吓坏了，转过身呜咽着逃走了。

小田鼠走到他们身边，声音尖细地说："谢谢你！你救了我的命！"

"理当如此，"铁皮人骄傲地回答说，"就算我没有心，我仍然想帮助所有需要帮助的人，哪怕只是个小动物。"

"什么，只是个小动物？我是田鼠皇后啊！"小田鼠愤慨地叫喊着。

"啊，很荣幸见到你，尊贵的皇后！"铁皮人说着深深鞠了个躬。

此时，上百只田鼠跑了出来，看到它们的皇后安然无恙，异口同声地喊

道："啊，皇后，太好了！我们都以为要失去您了！您是怎样逃过那只大野猫的追杀的呢？"

田鼠皇后说："是这位铁皮人帮了我，你们要感激他和他的朋友。我们都要为他服务！"接着它又问铁皮人："我能为你们做些什么呢？"

稻草人一直惦念着睡在几步之遥的狮子。他说道："有件事需要你们帮忙。你们能救出我们的狮子朋友吗？它现在正睡在罂粟花田里。"

"一只狮子！"田鼠皇后惊叫着说，"这太危险了！它会把我们全吃掉的。"

"啊，不，"稻草人说，"这是只胆小的狮子，不会伤害你们的。"

"胆小的狮子？这真是新鲜事，"皇后说，"我们信任你。但是我们要怎么做呢？"

"把你的臣民全都召集起来，让它们每个都带一根绳子。我的朋友铁皮人会造一辆车来运狮子。我们可以把狮子抬到车上，让田鼠们一起用力把车拉过来。"

于是铁皮人立刻造了一辆车，与此同时，数以千计的田鼠听到号令，从四面八方涌了过来。

这时多萝茜醒了。她睁开眼睛，眼前这番景象让她大吃一惊。铁皮人和稻草人欣喜地拥抱着她，然后把田鼠皇后介绍给她，又讲了讲他们救狮子的计划。所有田鼠都把绳子系到车上，多萝茜焦急地等在原地，其他人一起把车拉到熟睡的狮子那里，吃力地把狮子抬到了车上。上千只田鼠屏住呼吸一起用力，把车拉出了罂粟花田，回到多萝茜休息的地方。田鼠们从大车上解下绳子，互道再见后，与田鼠皇后一起迅速穿过草地跑走了。多萝茜和朋友们坐在狮子旁边，等着它醒过来。

狮子终于醒了过来。看到朋友们都在身边，它太高兴了。"我要吓死了，"狮子说，"我拼命跑，但还是睡了过去。你们是怎么把我救出来的呀？"他们给它讲了田鼠的事，狮子听完大笑着说："真想不到啊，我常常摆出十分强大可怕的模样，却险些被那么小的花夺走了性命，接着又被田鼠这么小的小动物救了命！我现在没事了，又能走了。我们要怎么办？"

多萝茜坚定地说："我们去找黄砖路，去翡翠城。"

大家一起动身，很快就找到了黄砖铺设的路。现在道路又是宽阔的了，路旁边围着的篱笆都漆成了亮丽的绿色。多萝茜注意到，就连田野里的人们都穿着绿色的衣裳，他们的房子也刷成了绿色。"我们肯定离翡翠城不远了。"多萝茜说。她怯生生地走向旁边田野里干活儿的小个子男人，问道："打扰了，我们要去翡翠城找伟大的奥兹，您能告诉我们还有多远吗？"

一身绿色衣服的小个子男人吃惊地打量着这个奇异的小团队，回答说："你们就快到了。可是你们认为奥兹会接见你们吗？要知道，他从来不允许任何人走到他面前。他整天坐在他宫殿中伟大的宝座上，但谁都不见，哪怕是侍奉他的人。"

"这太奇怪了，"多萝茜说，"可我们必须去见他。不然，我就无法回家了，狮子就无法得到胆量，稻草人就无法得到头脑，而铁皮人无法得到一颗心，永远不会再感受到幸福了。"

"我明白了，你们有无比重要的理由想见他。真心希望奥兹愿意帮助你们！祝你们好运！"和这位善良的绿衣小个子告别后，几个朋友继续前进。一身绿色衣衫的农夫没说错，刚走了一个多小时，他们就看见了一道绿色的光，在前面的天空中闪耀着。

他们已经抵达了翡翠城！

眼前是宏伟的绿色城墙，墙上装饰着翡翠，在阳光下绚丽夺目，就连稻草人那双画出来的眼睛都不免为之迷眩。他们走到城门旁，看到一个小个子男人站在那里，从头到脚的穿戴都是绿色的。这个绿衣人开口问道："你们来翡翠城有什么事？"多萝茜说："我们来这里是要拜访伟大的奥兹。"听到这个回答，小个子男人十分吃惊。"我守卫城门已经很多年了，从来没有人要求见伟大有力的奥兹巫师！我觉得……我不知道这可不可能，如果你们提出愚蠢的要求，打扰了奥兹巫师睿智神秘的冥想，也许他会发怒的。"

"但是，我们的要求并不愚蠢，它们十分重要！"多萝茜说，"而且有人告诉过我们，奥兹是位好巫师。"

"他的确是好巫师，翡翠城被他治理得井井有条。你们要求我领你们去见他，那我别无选择，只能带你们去他的宫殿。但你们必须先戴上眼镜。"说完，他拿起一个大盒子，给每个人发了一副又大又滑稽的眼镜，就连托托也戴上了眼镜。"为什么我们必须戴眼镜呢？"狮子吃惊地问。守门人回答说："如果不戴眼镜，翡翠城灿烂的光芒会照瞎你们的眼睛。这城里的居民也必须日夜戴着眼镜。这座城刚建成时，奥兹就下了这样的命令。"他用一把小锁把多萝茜戴好的眼镜锁上，这样多萝茜就不能随意把眼镜取下来了。

他们全戴好眼镜后，守门人打开城门，带他们走到翡翠城的大街上。

这座城市真的太绚丽了，如果没有眼镜的保护，多萝茜的眼睛真的会被光芒刺瞎。街道两边的房屋全都装饰着翡翠，房屋的窗户全都是绿色的，街道也是绿色的，街上来来往往的人们都穿着绿色的衣服，他们吃惊地看着守门人身后奇特的小团体。

多萝茜他们终于来到了奥兹的宫殿。与其他建筑相比，宫殿的光芒更为璀璨。一名卫兵陪他们走到觐见室，对他们说："在这里等我，我会向伟大的奥兹禀报你们的到来。"过了片刻，卫兵从里面走了出来，他们连忙跑上前去。"你见到奥兹了吗？"多萝茜问。"当然没有！我从来没见过他，但我和他讲了你们要见他，他起初很愤怒，接着又问了你们的相貌，我提到你的红鞋子后，他就决定接见你们。小女孩，你先进来吧。"说完，他不等多萝茜回答就转身打开门。多萝茜有点害怕，跟在后面一言不发地走了进去。

那是个很大的圆屋子，太阳般明亮的灯光从高高的屋顶照下来，照得墙上的翡翠闪闪发光。最让多萝茜惊奇的是宝座上那颗巨大的头颅，它就像巨人的头一样大，然而没有身体支撑它，更没有手脚。头颅上没有头发，只有眼睛、鼻子和嘴巴。

多萝茜在惊诧中凝视着那颗头颅。头颅开口说话了："我是伟大而可怕的奥兹。你是谁？为什么要来找我？最重要的问题是，你是从哪里得到的红靴子？"多萝茜小声回答说："我叫多萝茜。我来自堪萨斯州，我来请求帮助，想请你送我回家。这靴子不是我的，是东方邪恶女巫的。我的屋子恰巧落在她身上，把她砸死了。"

巨大的头颅看了她一会儿，又说道："在我这片国土上，人要得到什么东西都必须付出代价。运用神奇的魔力送你回堪萨斯州，这事情太不寻常了，如果你想让我帮你，就必须先为我做一件事。你帮我，我再帮你。你去杀死那个西方的邪恶女巫吧。""但是我做不到！"多萝茜大吃一惊，高声说道。那头颅说："你当然能做到，你已经杀掉了东方的邪恶女巫。去按我说的做吧，然后我就会帮你。"听到这些话,多萝茜开始失望地哭泣。她一生从来没伤害过任何人,又怎么去杀死那个邪恶的女巫呢?况且奥兹都无法打败那个女巫。

"我最后要说的就是,"奥兹说,"现在你可以去和你的朋友商量了。只要西方邪恶女巫还活着,我就不会见他们,更不会听他们的请求。"

多萝茜闷闷不乐地离开觐见室,把奥兹的话告诉了她的朋友们。"我们没希望了。"最后她说。"该怎么办呢?"她问几个朋友。狮子说:"我只有一个选择,就是找到西方邪恶女巫,把她消灭,否则我就永远不会有胆量了。""我就永远不会有心了。"铁皮人说。"而我,就不会得到我最渴望的头脑了。"稻草人说。多萝茜停止了哭泣,低声说道:"我真的不想伤害任何人,哪怕这是回到爱姆婶婶身边的唯一途径。不过,好吧,我们试一试吧。"就这样,他们决定第二天出发。

第二天清晨,他们离开了翡翠城,向西方邪恶女巫的领地进发。西方邪恶女巫只长了一只眼睛,但是那只眼睛非常强大,能看到十分遥远的地方。她很早就发现了多萝茜、狮子、稻草人和铁皮人正朝她城堡的方向走来。他们离得还很远,但是已经越过了边境,进入了她的地盘。这让她感到很愤怒。

她吹响了挂在脖子上的一个银哨子,身边立刻出现了一大群乌鸦,领头的是乌鸦王后。女巫命令道:"我要你们去把那些陌生人撕成碎片!飞到他们那里去,啄出他们的眼睛,阻止他们前进!"乌鸦群黑压压地飞向多萝茜和她的同伴。看见它们飞来时,稻草人站了出来,很自信地说:"这次我来战斗,交给我吧,不要担心,我不会让任何一只乌鸦伤害到你们！"于是他们在稻草人身后躺下来，稻草人伸出手臂上下挥舞着。乌鸦们看见他都很害怕，但是乌鸦王后说："那只不过是个稻草人，你们怕什么？跟我来！"她朝稻草人俯冲过去，但是稻草人手臂飞旋，把她甩到树上撞死了。另一只乌鸦冲向稻草人，稻草人依法炮制。他就这样打败了四十只乌鸦的轮番进攻，让那些乌鸦都送了命。

西方邪恶女巫看到发生的事情，非常愤怒。她吹了两次银哨子，招来了一群黑色的大蜜蜂。"把那些陌生人都蜇死！"女巫命令道。蜂群发出巨大的嗡嗡声，飞向朝着城堡前进的多萝茜和她的朋友们。第一个看到它们飞来的是狮子，但是稻草人又想出了个办法，他对铁皮人说："把我身体里的稻草拿出来，盖在多萝茜、托托和狮子身上，蜜蜂就蜇不到他们了。"铁皮人按他说的做了。黑色蜜蜂飞到他们这里时只发现了铁皮人。它们扑过去蜇铁皮人，但是刺扎到铁皮人身上就都折断了，根本伤不到铁皮人。蜜蜂蜇人之后自己也活不成了。多萝茜和狮子帮铁皮人把稻草重新放回稻草人的身体里，又继续往城堡走。看到黑色蜜蜂都死掉了，邪恶女巫更是生气，把牙齿咬得咯咯响。

她又一次抓起哨子，用力吹了三下，叫来了一群体形巨大的恶狼。铁皮人最先听到恶狼从林中冲了过来，他对朋友们说："这次我来战斗！你们站在我的后面，让我来面对它们。"他拿起磨得锋利的斧头，当第一头狼恶狠狠地奔过来时，铁皮人挥起斧头砍到狼身上。就这样，一匹又一匹恶狼倒在了他的斧头下。看到恶狼也无法阻止他们，邪恶女巫决定使用她的金冠。这顶金冠有一种魔力，可以召唤出一批飞猴，飞猴能服从召唤者的一切命令。但是这些奇怪的动物最多只能服从三次召唤。邪恶女巫已经用过两次魔力金冠，现在只剩下一次机会了。最后她决定动用金冠的力量。

她把金冠戴在头上，念出了咒语。空中立刻传来了隆隆声，接着是很多对翅膀拍动的声音。从云层中飞出了一群长着翅膀的大猴子，其中最大的

一只猴子凑近女巫，说道："这是你第三次召唤我们，也就是最后一次。你有什么命令？""我想要你们除掉那些野蛮的入侵者，他们竟胆敢擅入我的领地。把他们都杀死，除了狮子。我想让那头狮子给我拉车。"猴子们飞了起来，很快就飞到了多萝茜和她的朋友们赶路的地方。飞在前面的几只先捉住了稻草人，把他身体里的稻草全都拽出来抛到树上。其他飞猴捉住了铁皮人，飞到一处很深的山谷，把他扔了下去。他摔得那么重，连呻吟的力量都没有了。接着，飞猴甩出绳子捆住了狮子，准备把它带到女巫的宫殿。最后，它们恶狠狠地扑向多萝茜，却看见北方女巫留在多萝茜额头的那个吻，于是停了下来，决定把多萝茜一起带回宫殿。领头的飞猴王说："我们不敢伤害这个小女孩，因为她受到了善良女巫的保护，我们只能把她留给西方女巫了！"它们很小心地把多萝茜和狮子带回了城堡。"我们已经听了你的三次吩咐，"飞猴王对西方邪恶女巫说，"再也不要召唤我们了！"

邪恶女巫也看到了多萝茜额头闪闪发亮的记号，那是北方善良女巫留下的，她清楚，就连她自己也不能伤害这个小女孩。她低下头，看见了多萝茜脚上的红鞋子。她还以为多萝茜也是个巫师，拥有神奇的魔力，不禁吓得浑身发抖。但是她又注意到多萝茜的眼睛里流露出了纯洁和恐惧，显然这个小女孩并不知道这双鞋具有神奇的魔力，因此邪恶女巫决定一有机会就把这双鞋偷过来。

她把狮子关进了一个大笼子，又叫多萝茜去厨房刷锅扫地，自己则开始制订计划，要把魔力鞋偷走。最后她想出了一条诡计。她在大门和厨房之间系了根绳子，然后施了魔法，让人看不到这根绳子。多萝茜走过去时被隐形绳子绊倒了，一只鞋从脚上甩了出去。女巫立刻抢走了这只鞋，穿到自己脚上。多萝茜喊道："把鞋还给我！"女巫大笑着说："现在这只鞋是我的了，以后我还会把另一只鞋也拿走！"这句话把多萝茜气坏了，她拿起旁边的一桶水，泼到了女巫头上。老女巫立刻发出一声惊恐的尖叫，接着她的身体就开始融化！这意想不到的情形令多萝茜无比惊愕。

"你都干了些什么啊！"女巫哀号道，"你怎么知道只有水能要我的命？""我，我很抱歉，我，我不知道。"多萝茜结结巴巴地说。眼看着女巫一点点融化，就像水中的糖，多萝茜吓呆了。伴随着最后一声尖叫，女巫化成了石板上的一摊没有形状的深色的东西。多萝茜鼓起勇气，用更多的水把地冲干净，然后捡起女巫抢走的那只鞋，重新穿到自己脚上。

她跑出去把狮子从笼子里放出来，告诉它：

"西方邪恶女巫已经死了！"

听到这个消息，胆小的狮子开心地吼叫起来。两个朋友当下做了决定，要告诉被邪恶女巫奴役的温基人，他们已经自由了。能够重获自由，温基人非常高兴，当晚就举行了盛大的庆祝活动，以感谢多萝茜。但是多萝茜并没有那么开心，她想到了铁皮人和稻草人。

"我们如果能救他们该多好！"她叹着气说道。

那些温基人说，他们愿意帮助多萝茜搜救铁皮人和稻草人。于是多萝茜和一小队温基人立刻出发了。

他们找了两天，才在山谷底部发现了铁皮人，他几乎摔烂了，身上全都是锈。多萝茜看到他的样子，不禁哭了起来，但是一个温基人安慰她说："我们中间有些手艺非常好的铁皮匠，他们肯定知道怎么救你的朋友。"

铁皮匠们来了，立刻动手把铁皮人身上凹进去的地方弄平，给铁皮人的关节上油。一连三天三夜，他们都在锤击、抛光、焊接，直到铁皮人终于恢复原样，又能走过去见多萝茜了。

多萝茜紧紧地拥抱着他，接着又说："如果稻草人能与我们在一起就好了。"他们决定第二天去找稻草人。

最后他们终于找到了挂着稻草人的稻草和衣裳的那棵树。树很高，但是

铁皮人毫不气馁。他举起新斧头，很快就砍倒了那棵树，稻草落了一地。温基人把稻草都拾了起来，耐心地把稻草人的衣服缝好，把稻草一点点填充进去。稻草人复活了，多萝茜和铁皮人他们高兴得一会儿哭一会儿笑。

稻草人听他们讲完发生的事情后欢呼道："那女巫死了，我们可以返回翡翠城，请奥兹兑现他的承诺了！"多萝茜提议说："那我们明天就动身去翡翠城好不好？"几个朋友立刻表示赞同。

温基人恳求铁皮人留下来管理这片土地。铁皮人觉得这个提议不错，于是答应他们，只要奥兹能让他重新拥有一颗心，他就立刻回来。温基人送给几个朋友很多礼物。送给多萝茜的礼物是最贵重的，因为多萝茜拯救了他们。那礼物就是女巫的金冠。他们告诉多萝茜，使用金冠可以召唤三次飞猴。多萝茜对金冠没什么兴趣，她说："我不是女巫，我不知道能用这种魔力做什么！"但是稻草人说："我们可以用它召唤飞猴，让它们把我们驮到翡翠城，这样很快就会见到奥兹了。"多萝茜觉得这主意不错，于是念出了金冠上的咒语，头顶的天空顷刻乌云密布，紧接着，飞猴们从云层中冒了出来。

飞猴王深深鞠了一躬，问道："您有何吩咐？"

"我们想去翡翠城。"多萝茜回答。

"我们送你们去！上来吧！"多萝茜和她的几个朋友坐到飞猴背上，升到了空中。多萝茜从未想过，在空中飞行会如此愉快，她只觉得旅途太短，因为没过一会儿，他们就看到了翡翠城那璀璨的城墙。

四个朋友和小狗托托又戴上了守门人给的眼镜，走进城去见奥兹。他们来到宫殿，卫兵看到他们，目瞪口呆。这些奇怪的人居然杀死了可怕的西方女巫？他必须赶紧去通报强大的奥兹！卫兵进去向奥兹禀报，几小时后才回来，请四位来客一起进觐见室。

他们都以为奥兹还是上次出现在多萝茜面前的样子，可是他们大吃一惊，因为房间里空无一人，只传来一个雷鸣般的声音。"我是伟大而可怕的奥兹。你们为什么要来找我？"四个朋友走到空荡荡的宝座前面，多萝茜说道："我们来请求你兑现承诺！你说过，如果我们杀死了西方女巫，就会满足我们的愿望！"狮子想对多萝茜表示支持，于是发出了一声长长的吼叫，吓得小托托蹿了起来，一下撞倒了角落里的屏风。他们大吃一惊，因为屏风后面躲着一个满脸皱纹、又矮又老的秃顶男人。多萝茜问道："你是谁？""我是……我是奥兹，伟大而可怕的奥兹。"那矮小的老人结结巴巴地说。四个朋友惊愕地看着他。

"我以为你就是个大脑袋，"多萝茜轻声说，接着又愤怒地拔高了嗓门，喊道，"你还有哪些事撒了谎？你到底是不是个巫师？""亲爱的孩子，冷静！这就是我本来的样子，我承认，我是个冒牌货。"他笑着说。"但我看到过你！看到过那颗大大的头！那是怎么回事？"多萝茜问道。"那只不过是我的一种把戏。那头是厚纸造的，我用一根线拉动眼睛和嘴。灯光的作用加上你的恐惧，就骗过你了。"他回答。"那你到底是谁？"稻草人问道。于是奥兹开始讲述他的故事。"多萝茜，我出生的地方离你在堪萨斯州的家乡不远，我是在马戏团里长大的，后来成了热气球驾驶者，要乘坐热气球升到空中吸引观众。有一天我升到空中后，热气球的绳子断了，热气球飘到了云上面，被强风推动着飘到了这里。等我终于又落到地面时，就落在了这个地方，人们看见我从空中降落，就以为我是一个伟大的巫师。我任由他们这样想。他们恳请我治理这个地方，我答应了。我命令他们修建了翡翠城，为了使它名副其实，又命令所有的人都戴上绿眼镜。""为什么呢？难道这座城的颜色不是翡翠色的吗？"多萝茜吃惊地问。

"不是，这是座美丽的城市，但是让它呈现出翡翠色的，是眼镜的绿色镜片。

这也是我的一个把戏。你看，我认为我是个好心的人，但真不是个像样的巫师！"奥兹回答。

"那你允诺给我们的礼物呢？"铁皮人大声问道，"我永远不会有一颗心了吗？"奥兹看着多萝茜的朋友们，过了好久才回答："好吧，铁皮人，你们想要的东西我都能给你们，就从一颗心开始吧。""我太激动了！"铁皮人说。奥兹在身后的大箱子里翻找了一阵。"首先，我要在你的铁皮胸膛上剪个小洞，嗯，剪好了，然后我们把这个放进去！"奥兹边说边给铁皮人看一颗丝绸织成的漂亮的心。"这是颗善良美好的心。"说完，他把这颗心牢牢安放在铁皮人的胸膛里，又把剪开的方形小洞补好。"好啦，现在你感觉怎么样？"他问道。铁皮人深受感动，回答道："感觉比以前不知道要好多少倍，我简直描述不出来。"

"现在轮到你了，稻草人。请坐上那椅子，让我看看你的头。"说完，奥兹走了过去，戳着稻草人的头，观察了好长时间，然后点了点头，把稻草人的头拆了下来。他往那颗头里塞了些麦麸、图钉和针，把它们和稻草混合好，然后把头缝了回去。"你觉得怎么样？"多萝茜问稻草人。"非常聪明！"稻草人严肃地回答。

现在轮到狮子的胆量了。奥兹从一个旧柜子顶上取下一个金色的瓶子，把半瓶液体倒在碟子里。"这是胆量的精华，"他解释说，"把它喝下去，你的愿望就实现了。"狮子毫不犹豫地喝光了碟子里的药水，舔了舔胡须回味着，心想：药水很好喝，原来这就是胆量啊，味道有点像橘子水。"现在你觉得怎么样？"奥兹问。"充满胆量了！"狮子摇了摇鬃毛，回答说。

奥兹看着铁皮人、稻草人和狮子，向他们分别表示了祝贺。他不禁暗自发笑，心想：我这么容易就让他们相信，他们得到了我的馈赠，殊不知他们想要的东西其实是自身早已拥有的啊！但是，要把多萝茜送回家，可真不是件容易的事！奥兹突然想出了个主意。这有些冒险，但是值得一试！奥兹让多萝茜耐心等待三天。

第四天早晨，就在多萝茜几乎放弃希望时，奥兹叫她过去。她走进觐见室，奥兹对她说："亲爱的孩子，我想我找到把你带出这片土地的办法了。""回堪萨斯州吗？"多萝茜急切地问。奥兹回答说："去哪里我并不确定。有很大风险，但这是唯一的办法。我想到的是，我是乘坐热气球来到这里的，你是被旋风带到这里的，所以我相信，从空中走是我们唯一的办法！跟我来，我给你看看我造出了什么！"奥兹牵起多萝茜的手，领着她来到宫中的花园。"一个热气球？"多萝茜指着花丛间那丝绸织造的巨大的绿色气球，发出了惊叹。"我不知道怎么控制热气球啊！"多萝茜有些害怕地说。"但我知道！"奥兹眨了眨眼回答。"你的意思是说，你要和我一起走，真的吗？"多萝茜问道。"是真的！我已经厌倦了这样的伪装，厌倦了躲在这房间里。我不敢离开房间，担心人们会发现我和他们认为的不一样。我并不是个强大有力的魔法师。我真的愿意和你一起回堪萨斯州，我宁愿回到马戏团工作。因此，明天，强大的奥兹将向他的臣民告别，而我们将离开这里。"

第二天早晨，翡翠城的全体百姓都聚集到热气球旁边，来亲睹这非凡的事件。多萝茜对朋友们说了再见，流着泪和他们拥抱了很久。

奥兹给热气球充好了气，转身对他的臣民说："现在，我要去拜访我住

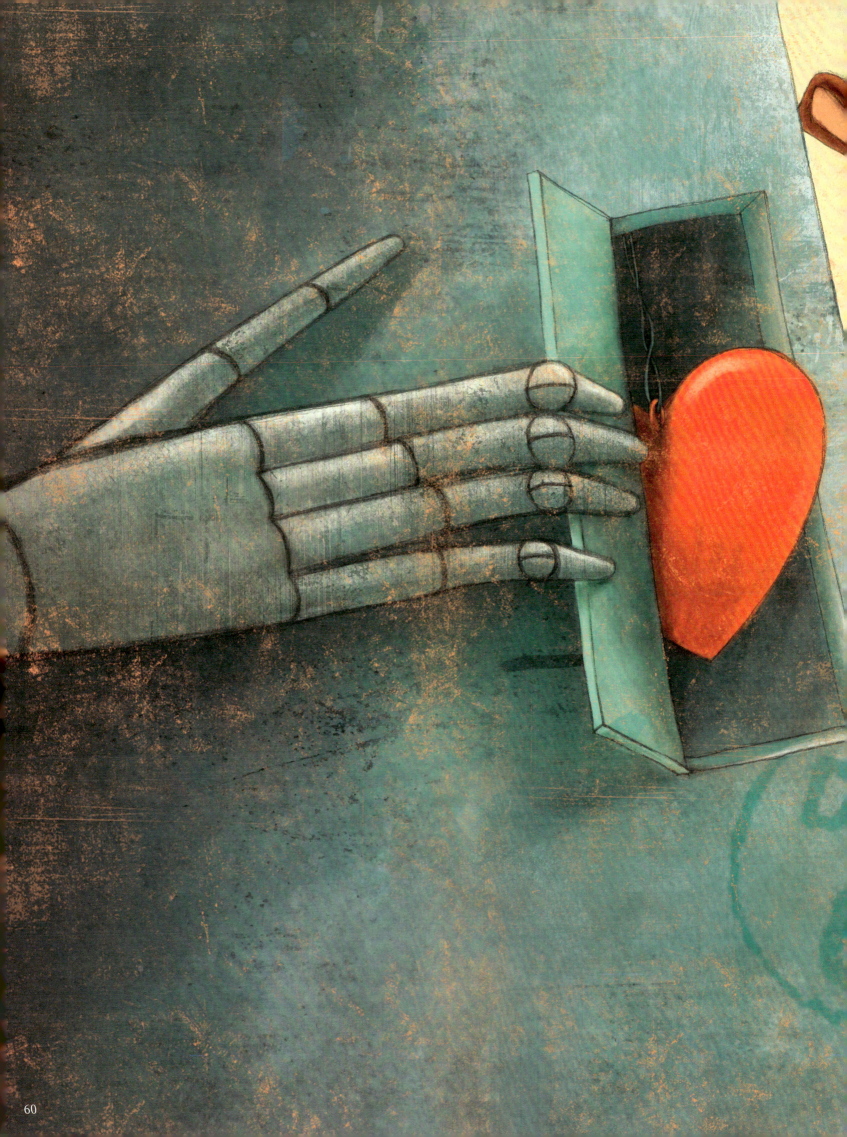

在云中的兄弟了。我离开后稻草人将代替我领导你们。他睿智而善良，我命令你们服从他，就如同你们服从我一样。"奥兹还没有说完，突然刮起了一阵大风。"多萝茜，快过来！"奥兹叫道。但是多萝茜没能及时跨进热气球下面的篮子……哗啦！固定热气球的绳子断了，热气球飘了起来，丢下了多萝茜。

"回来啊！"多萝茜高声叫道，"我也要上去！我要和你一起走！"

"我回不去了，亲爱的孩子，对不起！再会！"奥兹喊道。

绿色的热气球越升越高，很快就消失在云朵后面了。那是多萝茜最后一次见到伟大的奥兹巫师，我们只知道他平安地回到了家乡，或许现在还在马戏团里运用他那些技巧，让观众为他着迷呢！

翡翠城的百姓们久久地仰望着云端，满怀爱戴地感叹道："奥兹对我们太好了，离开时又留下睿智的稻草人来领导我们。"但是多萝茜回家的希望破灭了，她悲伤地哭了。她如此忧伤，铁皮人也为之动容，明知自己会生锈，还是难过得流下泪来。稻草人也感到悲伤，他邀请朋友们在宫殿里聚会，安慰多萝茜，同时也讨论一下那天发生的事情。

　　稻草人坐在他的宝座上，说道："想想吧，不久以前我还被吊在田间的木杆上面，现在却生活在这个漂亮的地方，这座美丽的城市，我还成了它的领导者。我简直不敢相信会有这样的好运气。"他接着又说："如果多萝茜愿意留在翡翠城中，我们就可以一起在这里快乐幸福地生活了。"

　　"但是我不愿意留在这里，"多萝茜难过地大声说，"我想回到爱姆婶婶和亨利叔叔身边！"

　　"我们怎么才能帮助她呢？"狮子问。

　　稻草人决意好好想个办法。由于他拼命地思考，脑袋里的钉子和针都要在脑壳上戳出孔洞了。最后他开口说道："为什么不召唤飞猴呢？"

　　听到这个建议，多萝茜精神一振，快活地说："真是好主意！稻草人，你新获得的头脑运转得真棒。"这还是奥兹离开后她第一次露出了笑容。

她戴上金冠，念咒语召唤飞猴王。那群飞猴立刻从窗户飞进来，站到她面前。"这是你第二次召唤我们来了，"飞猴王说，"你有何吩咐？""我想回到堪萨斯州，我叔叔和婶婶家里。你们能帮我穿过那片大沙漠吗？"飞猴王摇了摇头，说："抱歉，我办不到，我们只属于这个地方，不能离开。""那就没有人能帮助我了。"多萝茜的眼泪又一次从面颊流下，她伸手擦干了泪水。"或许甘林达能帮你。"飞猴王回答。"谁是甘林达？"铁皮人问。"她是南方女巫。在翡翠城周围土地的四个统治者中，她是最有力量的。她领导着桂特林人。她的宫殿就在沙漠边缘，但是到那里并不容易。去南方的路充满危险，野兽出没，还有很多奇异的生物。祝你好运！"说完这些话，飞猴王就从窗户飞走了。

"我要和多萝茜一起去，何况我多亏有她才得到了胆量。"狮子声明说。"这倒是真的，如果没有她，我现在仍然站在那树林里生锈，动都动不了。我要一起去！"铁皮人做出了决定。"我们一起去。"稻草人说。"我的朋友们，谢谢你们！"多萝茜十分感激地轻声说。于是她停止了哭泣，站了起来，把衣服弄平整，又说道："我想尽快动身。"

就这样，几个朋友很快又上路了。

他们来到城门口，守门人摘下他们的眼镜，祝他们旅途顺利，又对稻草人说："您会很快回来吧？您是我们新的领导者，我们需要您的智慧！"

稻草人安慰他说："只要多萝茜找到回家的路，我立刻就回来。"

四个朋友说笑着走向南方……

阳光照耀，多萝茜再一次满怀着回家的希望，铁皮人和稻草人都很开心，因为自己能帮到她。狮子和托托在点缀着野花的原野上自由奔跑，满心欢喜。

他们一直走到一片密林前面，在那里停了下来。

他们需要找到穿过密林的路。稻草人走到一棵大橡树旁边，刚刚弯腰要从树枝下走过去，树枝就弯了下来，缠住了他的身体，把他从地面举起来，头朝下扔到了草丛中。稻草人没受伤，但是那些树枝又抓住了托托，托托痛苦地叫了起来。铁皮人走上前去，勇猛地挥起了斧头，用力一劈，砍断了那根树枝。

那棵大橡树立刻举起了所有的树枝拼命摇动着，就像在诉说自己的愤怒和痛苦。

四个朋友从树下安然无恙地跑了过去。

多萝茜紧紧抱住托托，确定托托没受伤后，与朋友一起穿过森林。这之后再没有树攻击他们。

"为什么呢？那棵大橡树为什么要阻拦我们呢？"多萝茜惊魂未定地问道。

"我认为，那棵树是这片树林的守卫者，"铁皮人说，"它有特殊的力量，任务就是挡住陌生人。"

四个朋友在思考中穿过树林，一直跑到了树林的边界，眼前的景象让他们更加吃惊。

一堵高墙挡住了他们的去路，墙就像用整块白瓷砖砌的。

多萝茜问："现在我们怎么办啊？"

铁皮人说："我们需要个梯子。"于是他开始砍下一些树枝做木梯，同时多萝茜、稻草人和狮子继续打量这道奇怪的墙。

稻草人沉思良久后说道："我真想不出这墙的材料是什么。"

铁皮人回答说："让你新得到的头脑休息一下吧，不用多想墙的事情。有了梯子，我们就能爬上去，看看墙那边有什么了。"梯子做好了，铁皮人把梯子竖了起来。它看起来摇摇晃晃，但是足够高，可以让他们几个都爬到墙头。

墙那边的情形让他们瞠目结舌。稻草人的头刚越过白墙，就惊呼道："啊呀！"接着他爬上去坐在了墙上。多萝茜爬上墙头一看，也惊呼道："啊呀！"狮子和铁皮人也爬了上去，他们望见了一片奇异的景象：在那瓷托盘一样平滑、雪白的大地上，散布着完全用瓷盖起来的房屋，屋子都漆成了鲜艳的颜色。就连那些动物似乎也都是用瓷做的。但是最令人称奇的是这奇异国度里的居民。几个朋友看到了穿着华丽衣服的公主，穿着轻薄短裙的舞者，戴着镶满宝石的王冠的王子，顶着尖帽子的小丑。多萝茜甚至看到了一条像托托一样的小狗，他们全都是用瓷做的。

几个朋友从墙上跳下去，一条小狗向托托跑过来。托托友好地碰了碰它的鼻子，想邀它和自己一起玩耍，然而这小小的瓷狗跌倒了，摔断了尾巴。"看看你们做了些什么啊！"一个牧羊女喊道，"你们弄断了我的狗的尾巴！现在我只能带它去修理店，把尾巴黏回去。"多萝茜回答说："我十分抱歉。"她抱紧了托托，免得它再惹出更多麻烦。"我们必须十分小心，"铁皮人说，"不然我们又会弄伤这些娇小脆弱的生灵。"可是他们没走多远，狮子就险些撞上一个衣着华美的公主。"当心！"纤小漂亮的瓷公主叫道，"我真的不想让我漂亮的脸上出现裂纹。""你太美了，"多萝茜说，"你愿意和我一起去堪萨斯州吗？你可以在爱姆婶婶的壁炉装饰架上生活。如果你愿意，可以坐进我的篮子……""绝对不愿意，这会让我非常不开心，"瓷公主气愤地说，"你要知道，这里是我们的家园，我们在这里生活，非常心满意足。我们可以随意活动，随意谈天。但是如果离开这片土地，我们的关节就会变得僵硬，浑身冰冷，只能笔直地站着供人赏玩。当然，那些把我们摆在架子上或桌子里的人喜欢这样，但我们不喜欢！"

这个回答出乎多萝茜的意料，她高声说："我永远不想让你不开心！所以只好说再会了。我保证，我们会立刻离开，免得给你们带来更多损失。"他们继续前进，小心翼翼地穿过这个瓷器国。路上的人和动物都尽量躲开他们，担心会被他们弄碎。走了几小时后，这些旅行者又遇到了一堵瓷墙，那是这个瓷器国度另一面的边界。这堵墙没有先前那堵高，他们站到狮子背上翻了过去，而后狮子纵身一跃，跳过了这堵墙。他们就这样离开了这个奇特的国度。稻草人说："我一直以为，身体由破布和稻草制成是很糟糕的事，今天才发现这还不算最糟的。瓷器人这么容易就会被打碎，真是太可怕了。"

走了一整天后，多萝茜非常疲惫，因此他们决定停下来休息。这时天已经黑了。第二天早晨，他们才看清自己所处的环境，原来他们已经走到了一片原始森林的边缘，森林里古木参天，他们以前从来没见过这么高大的树。

"这地方真漂亮啊！"狮子环视四周，眼里闪烁着喜悦的光芒。"我愿在这里度过一生，不知道这里还有没有其他野兽？"仿佛在回应它的话一般，森林里突然传出一种声音，好像许多野兽在齐声吼叫。他们走到森林中央的空地时，才明白了刚才听到的是什么声音，因为这里聚集着各种动物，足有数百只。"它们是在举行会议。"狮子说。老虎、熊、狐狸、狼，还有一些多萝茜不认识的动物，它们正在激烈地讨论着什么，似乎遇到了十分棘手的问题。看到狮子和它的朋友们时，这些动物都安静了下来。

一只母老虎跑过来，说道："欢迎你，万兽之王！你来得正是时候，请你帮我们战胜敌人，让这片森林重归和平吧。"狮子问道："出了什么事？""不久前，一个可怕的怪物来到这里，让这里成了恐怖世界。它在林中搜寻各种动物，找到了就捉住吃掉。它长得就像只大蜘蛛，身体与大象一样大。我们召开这个会议讨论怎样做，正开会时，你出现了。帮帮我们吧，只要战胜那个怪物，你就是我们的王！""我同意！"狮子说道。它一声怒吼，跳起来就去寻找那个怪物了。

狮子在不远的地方找到了那个怪物，它正在一棵树下酣睡，样子十分丑陋可怕。狮子感到很庆幸，因为自己现在已经获得了胆量，否则看到这样的怪物只会尽快逃开。狮子观察了一阵子，最终决定要战胜这个怪物，只能在它熟睡时出其不意地发起进攻。说时迟那时快，狮子一跃而起，扑到怪物背上，用有力的脚爪猛然一击，怪物瞬间身首异处。

　　狮子回到林中空地，骄傲地宣布说："怪物已经被杀死了，你们再也不用害怕了！"听到狮子的话，动物们都拜倒在狮子面前，接着齐声长吼，高兴地请狮子当它们的王。狮子答应它们，只要多萝茜能回到堪萨斯州，自己就回来统领它们。几个朋友重新上路。

　　他们走出森林，就看见一座峻峭的高山横在面前，山上堆着大块的岩石。"来吧，朋友们，这座山非常难爬，但我们别无选择。"稻草人说道。但是，他刚开始攀爬那些巨大的岩石，就听到一个声音在喊："站住！不允许你们从我们的山上爬过去。"

　　"是谁说的？"稻草人喊了回去。

从岩石后面走出来一个奇怪的人，个子特别高，像根柱子，头是大大的长方体，但是没有手臂。

稻草人想，没手臂的人拿什么来阻止别人呢？于是他撒腿往山坡上跑。那个怪人的脖子立刻伸长了，头向前弹射出来，快得犹如闪电一般，猛地击中了稻草人。稻草人滚下山来，那怪人的脖子缩回到身体里，头也回到了身上。紧接着，数百个和他一样的无臂射头人站了出来，不怀好意地旋转着他们的头。

铁皮人扶起稻草人，说道："和这些射头人对抗是没有用的，没有人能抗得住他们大头的锤击。"

狮子问道："那我们怎么办呢？"

稻草人想了一会儿，对多萝茜说："多萝茜，召唤那些飞猴吧，你还可以最后命令它们一次。"

"好主意，我这就召唤它们。"多萝茜回答说。

她戴上了金冠，念着咒语。过了片刻，飞猴王飞出云层，降落到她面前。"你有何吩咐？"猴王问道。多萝茜回答说："驮着我们飞过这座山，到南方女巫的城堡去。"飞猴们背起四个朋友，带着他们从山上飞过去，射头人拼命伸长脖子，把头朝他们弹射出去，但是却怎么也打不到他们。没过多久，飞猴就把多萝茜和她的朋友平安地送到了南方善良女巫甘林达的城堡门口。飞猴王对多萝茜说："这是你第三次召唤我们，也是最后一次了。再会了，祝你好运。"说完，飞猴就升了起来，消失在空中。多萝茜向飞猴挥手告别后，和朋友们一起走进了甘林达的城堡。

南方善良女巫甘林达在觐见室接待了他们。这个女巫很美丽，一头红色长发，一双温柔的蓝眼睛。她和蔼地注视着多萝茜，而后嫣然一笑，问道："孩子，我能帮你什么？"多萝茜把一切经过都告诉了南方善良女巫：她怎样被旋风带到奥兹国，怎样遇见了几个朋友，又与朋友一起经历了哪些冒险奇遇，以及她是多么渴望回家。"回家是我最大的愿望！现在爱姆婶婶肯定认为我碰到了可怕的事。你能帮我吗？"她带着希望问南方女巫。甘林达俯身向前，吻了吻多萝茜的额头，说道："我想我能帮你，但是作为回报，你要把这顶金冠送给我。"

"当然可以！给你吧，"多萝茜说，"戴上金冠，你就可以召唤三次飞猴。"

甘林达微笑着回答："我想我需要它们的帮助。"

接着她问稻草人："等到多萝茜回家后，你想做什么？"

"我要回到翡翠城去，"他回答说，"因为奥兹叫我做那里的领导者，那里的人们都喜欢我。"

"我要叫飞猴做的第一件事，就是把你带到翡翠城的大门旁，因为那里的人们需要你这样有智慧的领导者。"说完，甘林达又问铁皮人："多萝茜回家后你想做什么？"

铁皮人想了一会儿，最后说道："西方邪恶女巫死后，温基人对我很好，请我领导他们。我也喜欢那个地方，我想对我来说，能回到他们那里是最好的，然后我会去找我爱过的人。"

"我对飞猴的第二个命令就是把你送到温基人的家园。他们受了那么多年的奴役，你的善良和宽厚的心，可以带给他们幸福。"最后，女巫友善地问狮子："多萝茜回家后你想做什么？"

狮子微笑着回答："几天前我们路过了一座大森林，那里所有的动物都愿意以我为王。如果我回到那美丽的森林里领导它们，与它们一起生活，我会非常快乐。"

"那我会命令飞猴把你驮到你的森林中。那将是我第三次命令它们，也是最后一次了，之后我将把金冠还给飞猴王，让它和它的部下以后可以摆脱诅咒，自由自在地生活。"稻草人、铁皮人和狮子发自内心地感激女巫的善良。

多萝茜有些羞怯地说："你心地这么好，这么善良，还这么美丽！但你还没告诉我怎么才能回到堪萨斯州呢。"

"你的红鞋子会带你回家。你并拢脚，让双脚的鞋跟互相碰撞三次，就可以命令这双鞋子带你到任何你想去的地方。"甘林达又说，"如果你早就知道东方邪恶女巫这双鞋的魔力，那你在来到这里的第一天就可以回家了。"

"但是如果那样，我现在依然被吊在那片田地中间的杆子上，永远也不会有头脑了！"稻草人叫喊起来。"那我就永远是个胆小鬼了。"狮子说。"那我永远也不会重新得到一颗心了，我将一直孤独地站在森林中生锈。"铁皮人说着说着，情不自禁地流下了眼泪，尽管这对他的关节有害。多萝茜听到朋友们的话，被深深地打动了。

多萝茜紧紧拥抱着几个朋友，又向善良女巫甘林达表达了谢意。她抱起托托，把脚下红鞋子的鞋跟互相碰撞了三次，说道："带我回爱姆婶婶和亨利叔叔那里！"她身边的世界一瞬间就消失了，她飞到了空中，耳边只有呼啸的风声。

没过多久，一切突然又静止下来，多萝茜发现自己坐在了地上。她紧张不安地睁开眼睛看了看四周，然后大笑起来，欢呼道：

"托托，我们回家了！"

多萝茜终于可以再次拥抱亲爱的爱姆婶婶。

图书在版编目（CIP）数据

绿野仙踪 /（意）曼纽拉·阿德雷亚尼绘；（美）弗兰克·鲍姆著；李静滢译. —广州：广东人民出版社，
2023.3

（镜子书·新编经典童话绘本系列）

ISBN 978-7-218-16038-2

Ⅰ. ①绿⋯　Ⅱ. ①曼⋯　②弗⋯　③李⋯　Ⅲ. ①儿童故事—图画故事—意大利—现代　Ⅳ. ① I546.85

中国版本图书馆 CIP 数据核字（2022）第 175717 号

LÜYE XIANZONG

绿 野 仙 踪

［意］曼纽拉·阿德雷亚尼　绘　　　［美］弗兰克·鲍姆　著　　　李静滢　译　　　　版权所有　翻印必究

出 版 人：肖风华

责任编辑：寇　毅
责任技编：吴彦斌　周星奎

出版发行：广东人民出版社
地　　址：广州市越秀区大沙头四马路 10 号（邮政编码：510199）
电　　话：（020）85716809（总编室）
传　　真：（020）83289585
网　　址：http://www.gdpph.com
印　　刷：北京尚唐印刷包装有限公司
开　　本：1000 毫米 ×1250 毫米　1/16
印　　张：5　　　字　　数：46 千
版　　次：2023 年 3 月第 1 版
印　　次：2023 年 3 月第 1 次印刷
定　　价：78.00 元

如发现印装质量问题，影响阅读，请与出版社（020-87712513）联系调换。
售书热线：（020）87717307

馔®

出 品 人：许　永
出版统筹：林园林
责任编辑：寇　毅
特邀编辑：陈璐璟
装帧设计：李嘉木
印制总监：蒋　波
发行总监：田峰峥

发　　行：北京创美汇品图书有限公司
发行热线：010-59799930
投稿信箱：cmsdbj@163.com

官方微博

微信公众号

"镜子啊，墙上的镜子，谁是世界上最团结朋友的孩子？"

饙

THE WIZARD OF OZ

BASED ON THE MASTERPIECE BY

L. FRANK BAUM

ILLUSTRATIONS BY

MANUELA ADREANI

*Y*oung Dorothy's best friend was her little dog, Toto. Toto made the little girl laugh, and stopped her from becoming gray, like the rest of her world. The cabin where Dorothy lived with her aunt and uncle was sad and gray, just like the prairies all around it! But Toto had brown and white fur, a tail that never stopped wagging, and lively eyes that pleaded with Dorothy to play with him.

Today, though, the little girl did not want to play. Something strange was going on, she thought, watching Uncle Henry looking anxiously at the sky, which was darker than usual. In the distance the wind whistled. It blew ever harder, and soon it started to ripple the grass. Uncle Henry jumped to his feet: "Em, there's a tornado coming!" he cried to his wife. "Quick, into the cellar!"

Scared by the shouting, Toto jumped out of Dorothy's arms and hid himself under the bed, and Dorothy hurried to get him. In the meantime, it took Aunt Em only a glance out of the door to see the danger. She dropped the plate that she had been washing, ran to open the trapdoor in the middle of the room and started down the ladder into the cellar. "Come here, Dorothy, now!" she cried before disappearing underground.

Eventually, Dorothy seized Toto and went after her aunt. However, she had only got halfway across the room when something very strange happened. The howling of the wind became deafening and the cabin shook so violently that the little girl lost her balance. Sitting on the floor, Dorothy saw the house spin around twice and then rise into the air, flying ever higher, until it reached the very top of the tornado. Out of the window, the little girl could see the cows and horses that Uncle Henry had not managed to put into their stable flying alongside the house.

Toto did not like any of this at all. He started to run up and down the room, barking furiously and then, getting too close to the trapdoor, he fell in. For a long, terrifying moment, Dorothy thought she would never see him again, but she soon saw Toto's nose poking up. The strong wind had held him up and stopped him falling. Now Dorothy crawled to the trapdoor, helped the little dog to climb back in, and banged the door shut. With Toto in her arms, she sat on the floor without moving, listening to the howling of the wind all around her. For what seemed like forever, the little girl wondered whether the house would crash to the ground or whether the wind would smash it to pieces, but when she saw that nothing terrible had yet befallen her she grew calm and waited to see what would happen. At last, crawling across to her bed, she hugged Toto tight, closed her eyes and went to sleep, while the house, suspended in the air as if it were as light as a feather, was swept along all night.

Dorothy was woken with a jolt by a loud noise and such a loud cry that she fell out of her bed. Scared, the little girl opened her eyes

only when she felt Toto licking at her hand: the dog was more afraid than she was, thought Dorothy. The girl sat up and saw that the house was no longer spinning, the wind had dropped and, with it, the dark night had ended. The sun shone through the window, flooding the room with light.

Dorothy jumped down from the bed, ran to open the door and let out a cry of wonder at the marvelous scene that was laid out before her. The tornado had dropped the cabin down in a most beautiful place. Banks of brightly colored flowers dotted the countryside, and nearby ran a gurgling stream in which small birds washed their colorful feathers. Dorothy saw a small group of people coming along the path, calling out to her at the tops of their voices. There were three men and one woman, the strangest grownups that the little girl had ever seen. They wore tall, blue, cone-shaped caps with bells that tinkled gaily at every step. Their clothes were also blue, and so were their long beards and their pointy shoes. The little woman, however, wore a white dress decorated with stars that glittered like diamonds.

She came over to the cabin, while the others stayed behind her, suddenly daunted and a little scared.

The little woman bowed deeply and said, "Oh, most powerful sorceress, welcome to the land of the Munchkins! How can we ever thank you for killing the Wicked Witch of the East and freeing these people from slavery?"

Dorothy was speechless. Why had this little woman called her a sorceress? And what did she mean by saying that Dorothy had killed the Wicked Witch of the East? She had never hurt anyone. They must have mistaken her for someone else! She had to put them right. "You are very kind, but you must have mistaken me for someone else," Dorothy said hesitantly. "I have never killed anyone!"

"But your cabin has!" replied the little woman, pointing to the corner of Dorothy's house, where two feet in shiny red boots were sticking out.

"Oh, no! What have I done? How did that happen? I... I am truly sorry; I didn't do it on purpose! What can we do?"

"There's really nothing we can do, my dear," replied the little woman, smiling.

"But who was it?" asked Dorothy.

"It was the Wicked Witch of the East. For many, many years, she has enslaved the inhabitants of this place, the Munchkins. Now, these gentle people are free at last, and they want to thank you as is only right."

"Are you a Munchkin?" asked the little girl, who was still very confused. "No, but I am their friend and I hurried here from the land in the north where I live as soon as they sent for me.

I am the Witch of the North," replied the little woman.

"A witch? Are you a real witch?"

"Yes, my dear, but I am a good witch and everyone loves me. And I'm not the only one. There are four witches in the Land of Oz and two, those who live in the North and the South, are good. I'm certain of it, for I am one of them. But the witches that live in the East and the West are evil! Now that you have killed one, there is only the Wicked Witch of the West left. And there is Oz, of course, the great wizard," concluded the little woman.

"The wizard? There is a wizard too?" asked an astonished Dorothy. "And what did you say his name was?"

"His name is Oz, my child. He is a very powerful wizard, and he lives in the City of Emeralds and..."

Just then, the Munchkins, who up until then had not said a word, gave a shout and pointed at the corner of the cabin where a short while before the witch's feet had been sticking out.

"What's happening?" asked the Witch of the North. "Oh, yes, the wicked one was so old that she has shriveled up in the sun. All that remains are her red boots. Take them, my child, they are yours."

Fetching them and brushing off the dust, one of the Munchkins came up to Dorothy and offered her the boots. "The Witch of the East was very proud of those boots," he said. "Undoubtedly, they have magical powers, even if we don't really know what they are." Dorothy took the boots and thanked the Munchkin. She put them on her feet in place of her old, gray clogs, and then she looked up and said, "I very much want to go home. My uncle and aunt are bound to be worried about me. Could you help me to find the way?"

"I'm sorry," said the Witch of the North, "but I do not know where to tell you to go. In the East, there is a great desert which no-one can cross. In the North, too, there is an endless desert. I know it well because that is my home."

"The same goes for the South!" declared one of the Munchkins. "And they say that it's the same in the West. The desert surrounds the whole kingdom of Oz!"

"I think you'll have to stay with us, my child," concluded the Witch of the North.

Hearing these words, Dorothy started to sob. Toto went to her and whined, but not even the little dog could console the girl.

"Oh, my dear, don't cry, perhaps we'll find a way!" the little woman said. "It's simple, even if it will be a very hard and extremely dangerous journey!"

"What must I do?" asked Dorothy, drying her eyes.

"Go to the Emerald City! Perhaps Oz will help you. Certainly he is the only one who is powerful enough to do so!"

"And where is the Emerald City?" asked Dorothy in a whisper.

"Right at the center of the land. You must follow the road that is paved with yellow bricks. You can't miss it. The journey ahead is long. You must cross beautiful lands and terrible and frightening lands," explained the Witch.

"Will you come with me?" asked Dorothy hopefully.

"I cannot go to the Emerald City, but I will give you a kiss, and then no-one will dare to harm you." So saying, the little woman came up to Dorothy and gently placed a kiss on her forehead, and the spot where she did so immediately began to sparkle. "When you arrive at the City of Emeralds, ask for an audience with Oz. I am sure that he will be able to help you. Farewell, my child." The witch turned round three times and disappeared.

The three Munchkins said goodbye with a final bow and walked away.

"There, Toto, now we're alone. Are you scared? I am a little. But we must be brave and follow the yellow brick road to the Emerald City. Only there will we find out how to get back home. Are you ready to go?" The little dog fixed his black eyes on her, wagging his tail to show her he understood everything. Dorothy went back into the house, found a basket and took some bread from the cupboard. Then she closed the cabin door, tied the laces of the red boots and set out on her journey.

The sun shone high in the sky and little colored birds sang from the treetops, annoying Toto, who chased them, barking. Dorothy watched him with a smile and very soon she realized that she was no longer afraid.

Neither did she feel lonely, because she often came across Munchkin farmers working in the fields, and when they saw her pass by, the little blue men stopped work to come over and greet her with a bow, for everyone knew by now that it was she who had liberated them from the cruel witch. Every time, Dorothy stopped and returned their greetings with a smile, while Toto jumped around in circles barking merrily, astonishing the Munchkins, who had never seen a dog before.

After walking for more than an hour, Dorothy decided to stop for a rest, and she climbed onto a fence beside the road, beyond which there was a large cornfield, with, in the middle, a scarecrow tied to the top of a pole to keep the birds away.

Taking the bread out of the basket and giving Toto a piece, Dorothy started to eat, and as she ate, she looked at the scarecrow. There was something strange about it, but Dorothy could not put her finger on what it was. At first sight, it seemed to be a very normal scarecrow. It wore old clothes and worn-out boots, and its head was a small sack

stuffed with straw, on which someone had drawn eyes, a nose, and a mouth. Just as she was busy studying the painted face, Dorothy gave a start. The Scarecrow had winked at her!

"I must be mistaken, Toto! But..." Now the doll gave her a little nod with its head, and there was no doubt about it: it was asking her to come closer! Timidly, Dorothy slipped down from the fence and went into the field.

"Hello," said the Scarecrow, clearing his throat.

"Did you speak? Did you really speak?" asked Dorothy, full of astonishment.

"Of course I did! Do you want to chat a little with me? How are you?"

"I... I'm very well, I'm just a little surprised to hear you speak, that's all..." replied Dorothy. "And how are you?" she added politely.

"Not very well. I'm terribly bored. For weeks, I've done nothing but scare the crows, and this pole stuffed up my back is truly uncomfortable! Would you be able to get me down, please?" Dorothy went over to the doll and took him down from the pole. It was an easy task because his whole body was stuffed with straw and he was very light. "Thank you very much!" said the Scarecrow, starting to stretch, bend and turn.

"Now that's better, much better!" he concluded when he had finished his strange exercises. "I don't know how to thank you! And I don't even know your name: who are you?"

"My name is Dorothy, I came here from Kansas and... well, it's a long story. I'm going to the Emerald City to meet the great Oz and ask him to help me to get home," explained the little girl.

"Who is Oz?" asked the curious Scarecrow.

"What, you don't know?" asked Dorothy, surprised.

"No, I don't know anything. I'm stuffed with straw and I don't have a brain," replied the Scarecrow, shaking his head sadly.

"I'm very sorry!" exclaimed Dorothy.

"Do you think that if I come with you to the Emerald City, Oz would give me a brain?"

"I don't know, but if you want to you can come with me. It's worth trying, don't you think?"

"Absolutely! You know, I don't mind having my body, legs and arms stuffed with straw, because no-one can hurt me if they hit me, or prick me with a pin... but I miss having a brain very much. It's definitely very annoying to feel I'm a fool!"

Dorothy was sincerely moved. "You should definitely come with Toto and me!" she declared.

"Thank you," replied the Scarecrow gratefully. Dorothy helped him to climb the fence, and together they set out along the yellow brick road.

Toto did not like this development. He began to sniff suspiciously at his new traveling companion, growling softly. "Toto! Stop that!" Dorothy chided. "Don't worry, he never bites."

"Oh, but I'm not afraid," replied the Scarecrow cheerfully. "Even if he does bite me, he can't hurt me! There's only one thing that frightens me to death: a lighted match!" And so saying he strode out along the road, which at that very point entered a wood. But after a few steps, he stumbled in a pothole and fell flat on his face on the yellow bricks. Here, in truth the road was very rough, full of potholes made by the roots of the trees. Toto jumped over them and Dorothy went around them but the Scarecrow, who did not have a brain, walked straight ahead and tripped at every step. But he never hurt himself. Dorothy helped him get up and they went on, chatting as they walked.

"Can you tell me why you want to leave this beautiful country and go back to your gray Kansas?" asked the Scarecrow at one point. "I really don't understand it!"

"That's because you don't have a brain," replied Dorothy, trying not to offend her friend. "If you had one, you would know that there's no place like home."

"Well, this is all new to me. But it doesn't surprise me. I was made only a couple of weeks ago and I've never had a home. I have always been in the middle of that field, chatting with the crows. I remember one day, while I was complaining about the pole stuck up my back, one of them said to me that if I had even the tiniest brain I would have left that place a long way behind me. And so I understood that a brain is the most important thing that you can have, and I promised myself that I would do everything I could to get myself one. I can't wait to get to the Emerald City!

What are you doing?" he asked, seeing that Dorothy had sat down under a tree and was yawning. "I'm very tired, and it's getting dark... can we stop and sleep a little while?" asked the little girl, while Toto snuggled up to her. "Yes, of course, but wait, I have an idea," replied the Scarecrow, and he started to pull straw out of his shirt and spread it on the ground. "There! Lie down here and you won't get cold," he said when he had finished. Dorothy lay down, and, with Toto at her side, went straight to sleep. The Scarecrow, who was never tired, stood under a tree and waited for morning.

When the sun rose, Toto opened his eyes, yawned and hurried to wake his mistress by giving her a few quick little licks on her nose. Dorothy got up and saw the Scarecrow waiting for her quietly at the side of the road.

"Good morning! Can we go?" he asked her.

"Just a moment," replied the girl. "I would like to find some water."

"But why?"

"To wash with and to drink."

"Hmm... it must be really troublesome to be made of flesh! You have to drink, to wash, to sleep. But you have a brain, and it's worth all that bother if you can think," concluded the Scarecrow, nodding with conviction. Then he followed Dorothy, who had left the path and had gone in among the trees with Toto. The little dog seemed to know perfectly well where to find a spring, and soon he found a stream running with clear water where the girl could wash and drink. They were just returning to the yellow brick road when they heard a sound, like a sob, coming from the forest.

"What was that?" asked Dorothy, hurrying to take hold of Toto, who was growling.

"I really don't know," replied the Scarecrow. "But we can go and see!"

At that moment, they heard another moan coming from behind them. They turned around and walked toward the noise and, after a few steps, Dorothy saw something glinting among the trees.

Curious, the little girl started to run, but she stopped short as soon as she saw what it was shining, or rather, who! Next to a tall tree there was a man made entirely of tin. He was quite still, with an ax grasped in his two hands and poised above his head. His head, his arms and his legs were connected to his body by joints, but it seemed as if the tin man was quite unable to move, and that he was stuck in that uncomfortable position next to the tree. Dorothy walked all around him, staring at him in astonishment, and the Scarecrow too, who came up just at that moment, seemed very surprised. But Toto barked and snarled and growled, and more than once tried to bite the bizarre figure's leg, but in doing so hurt his teeth.

"Hello," said Dorothy at last. "Hmm... can you hear me?"

"Yes, yes, I hear you," replied the tin man.

"Did you moan?"

"Yes, I did. For more than a year I've been moaning, but no-one ever heard me or came to help me."

"We'll help you! But how? Tell me what to do!" replied Dorothy, moved by the man's sad voice.

"Oh, thank you! Down there is my hut, and on the table you will find an oil can. Bring it here and oil my joints, I beg you! I am so rusty that I can't move any more. But if you oil me well I will be as good as new!"

Dorothy ran to the hut, took the oilcan and hurried back to the tree.

"Here I am! Where are your joints?" she panted.

"First my neck," replied the Tin Woodman, and the little girl hurried to oil it well, but because it was so badly rusted the Scarecrow had to help him by gently moving the head from side to side until the Woodman could move it freely. "Now my arms and legs," and again the Scarecrow gently bent the joints that were rusted while Dorothy poured the oil on until the Tin Woodman was able to move freely. "I truly don't know how to thank you!" he exclaimed with a bow. "If it had not been for you, I would have been stuck for years, because no-one ever passes this spot! By the way: how come you are passing through these woods?"

"We are on our way to the Emerald City," replied Dorothy, "to seek the great Wizard of Oz. I want to ask him how to get back home and the Scarecrow wants him to put a brain in his head." The Tin Woodman was silent for a few seconds and then asked, "Do you think that Oz could give me a heart?"

"I don't know. But probably yes!" Dorothy added quickly seeing that the Tin Woodman was on the point of crying again. "If he can give the Scarecrow a brain, he can surely give you a heart." "Well, then, I will come with you!" said the Tin Woodman. "So you want a brain?" he continued, turning to the Scarecrow. "I had one once, but I don't want one anymore!"

I PROMISE YOU THAT IF I HAD TO CHOOSE BETWEEN A BRAIN AND A HEART, I WOULD PREFER THE LATTER BY A LONG WAY!

A heart is the most important thing in the world!" concluded the tin man.

"But why?" asked the Scarecrow. "I will tell you my story, and then you will understand." And as they walked through the forest, the Tin Woodman started to tell his story. "I was not always made of tin, I was a normal woodman until one day I met a Munchkin girl and fell in love with her. I could not wait to marry her, and so I started to work harder than I had ever worked before so that I could build a big house for us to live in.But the Munchkin girl worked in the palace of the Wicked Witch of the East, who did not want to let her go. So the Witch cast a spell on my ax, which suddenly slipped from my hand and cut off one of my legs.

I was desperate, as you can imagine, but the village tinsmith found a solution. He replaced the leg that was cut off with one made of tin, and so I returned to work. But within a few days the bewitched ax slipped once again and cut off my other leg and then both my arms. Again, the tinsmith saved me, replacing the missing parts with arms and legs made out of tin. I went back to cutting trees, until one day the bewitched ax cut off my head. At this point, I felt truly done for, but once again, the tinsmith managed to help me, making me a new head out of tin. I thought I had beaten the Wicked Witch, but one terrible day, the ax hit me on the chest. I ran to the tinsmith, who replaced it, but there was no way he could replace my heart and I lost all the love that I had felt for the Munchkin girl that I had wanted to marry.

My body shone in the sun and I could no longer be hurt, and this was enough for me for many years, until one day I was caught in a storm. I was drenched and my joints rusted, and so I was stuck in the *forest for a year. Being stuck for so long was horrible, but it did give me time to think. I realized that when I was in love I was happy; the happiest man in the world, but no-one can love without a heart. So I understood that my greatest loss was the loss of my heart. And this is why I want to ask Oz to give me one, and if he will, I will go back to the Munchkin girl and ask her to marry me."*

Dorothy and the Scarecrow listened carefully to the Tin Woodman's story, and they did not notice that the yellow brick road had become a narrow path, and that the forest was becoming ever thicker and darker.

Every now and then, there came strange grunts and mysterious sounds from the thick bushes, which made the girl's heart beat faster and frightened Toto, who trotted next to her and no longer strayed from her side.

All of a sudden, a terrible roar came out of the forest and a huge lion landed on the road with a great leap. With one paw, he knocked the Scarecrow over and then he hit the Tin Woodman, but to his enormous surprise he saw that his claws did not even scratch him. Angrily, he turned on Dorothy, but when Toto saw his mistress being threatened, he lunged at the lion, barking furiously.

The beast opened his mouth to bite the dog, but Dorothy ran up to him and slapped him on the nose with all her strength: "Don't you dare bite Toto! You should be ashamed of yourself! A big thing like

you biting such a little dog!" "But I didn't bite him," said the Lion, rubbing his nose where Dorothy slapped him. "No, but you tried! You're nothing but a coward!" replied the girl curtly. "Yes, I know, I'm a coward," replied the Lion, "I've always known, but what can I do?"

"For a start, you could avoid hitting the poor Scarecrow and knocking the stuffing of him!" declared Dorothy, who was still angry.

"He's stuffed! That's why I didn't hurt him! And he's made of metal?" asked the Lion, pointing to the Tin Woodman. "That explains why my claws didn't scratch him! And is he stuffed or made of metal?" he asked, pointing to Toto. "Him? Neither. He's an animal. He's my dog." "Oh! Now that I look at him, he is remarkably small! No-one would think to hurt him, except a coward like me, "concluded the Lion shaking his mane, and he was so sad and sorry that Dorothy could not continue to scold him.

"Maybe you could stop acting like a coward," she suggested. "I don't know how to do it, I was born this way. All the animals of the forest expect me to be brave, because the lion is the king of the animals, so I learned to roar very loudly to scare everyone, but if bears, tigers or elephants had ever tried to attack me, I would have run away. I can't help it, everything terrifies me!" concluded the Lion, wiping away a tear with the tip of his tail. "Every time I hear danger approaching, my heart pounds!"

"This means that you have a heart. You are very lucky for I don't have one anymore," interrupted the Tin Woodman.

"And I don't have a brain!" said the Scarecrow.

"And I want to go home. This is why we are going to the Emerald City: we are going to meet the Wizard of Oz and ask him for a brain, a heart and to send Toto and me back to Kansas," concluded Dorothy.

"If you have no objection, I will come with you and try to talk to this wizard, to ask him to give me courage. So long as I am a coward, I will always be unhappy." So once again, the friends continued their journey, with the Lion striding majestically alongside Dorothy.

They had been walking for less than an hour when they reached a large chasm, very wide and very deep, with steep sides and sharp staves at the bottom. It divided the forest in two as far as the eye could see. They could see the yellow brick road continuing on the other side, but it seemed impossible to reach it! *"What are we going to do?"* Dorothy asked anxiously.

"I think I can jump to the other side," said the Lion after studying the distance carefully.

"It's perfect! You can take us on your back one at a time," cried the Scarecrow. *"I'll go first, because I am made of straw and even if I fall it won't hurt."*

"Fall? Don't make me think about it, I'm scared enough as it is! Very

well, get on my back!"

The Scarecrow climbed on his back and grabbed two locks of his mane. The Lion crouched on the edge of the abyss and then, with a great leap, flew over the ditch and landed safely on the other side. "It was easy," he admitted, jumping back across. "Whose turn is it now?"

"I'll go!" said Dorothy, picking up Toto. A moment later, she seemed to be flying, and before she had time to be afraid, she found himself on the other side.

Finally, it was the turn of the Tin Woodman. Then they all sat down in safety for a few minutes waiting for the Lion to recover from all those mighty leaps, which had left him breathless and with his tongue hanging out. On that side of the chasm, the forest was dark and thick, and the little group of friends went slowly, waiting for the Tin Woodman as he cut the branches that barred their way.

After many hours, they had not gone very far when they found themselves at a second chasm but this one was so broad and so deep that the Lion knew at once that he could not cross it.

"If it were smaller, I could do it again in a single leap with you on my back, but I don't think I can jump so far!" exclaimed the Lion. "Brrr, I'm shaking with fear just to think of it!"

"I have an idea!" said the Scarecrow suddenly, "Look at that tree. It's huge! If the Tin Woodman can cut it down so that it falls across the gap we can use it as a bridge."

"That's a great idea! You might almost believe that you have a brain under all the straw that's stuffed into your head!" the Tin Woodman complimented him. "I'll get right to work."

"But hurry," whispered the Lion. "The Kalidahs live in this part of the forest."

"Who are the Kalidahs?" asked Dorothy.

"Monstrous beasts, with the body of a bear and the head of a tiger. They have long claws that terrify me!" explained the Lion.

In the meantime, the Tin Woodman had almost managed to cut down the giant tree with a few well-aimed blows of his ax. Then the Lion leaned his front paws against the trunk and pushed until, at last, the tree fell. "That's it, let's go!" They had just started to cross the bridge when they suddenly heard a tremendous grunt coming from the forest behind them, and quickly turned around. Running towards them were two huge beasts, with the body of a bear and the head of a tiger. "The Kalidahs!" cried the Lion, starting to tremble.

"Quick, across the bridge!" cried the Scarecrow.

Dorothy ran forward clutching Toto in her arms, followed by the Scarecrow and the Tin Woodman. The Lion stayed until last, and although he was trembling with fear, he stopped to confront the Kalidahs and give his friends time to get away. He closed his eyes and roared so loudly that Dorothy and the Scarecrow began to scream and even the Kalidahs stopped in amazement. A few moments later, however, they realized that they were larger and more numerous than the Lion, so they rushed forward and without a moment's hesitation jumped on the tree trunk to follow him.

"Run!" cried the Lion, "We're doomed! They'll rip us to pieces for sure! Quick, Dorothy, hide behind me."

"Wait!" shouted the Scarecrow. "I have an idea! Quick, Tin Woodman, cut the top off the tree at this point."

The tin man set right to work and with two great blows of his ax cut through the tree just as the Kalidahs were almost upon him. The makeshift bridge broke and fell into the abyss, taking the two beasts with it, and everyone breathed a sigh of relief.

"Those creatures frightened me so much that I can still feel my heart pounding in my chest," said the Lion.

"Oh," murmured the Tin Woodman, "I too would like to hear that." After this adventure, the travelers continued on their way, and because they were anxious to get out of the forest as soon as possible, they began to walk so fast that Dorothy had to climb on the back of the Lion so as not to be left behind. Fortunately, after a couple of hours' walking, the trees became less dense and the forest gave way to a wonderful orchard, which the friends crossed, jumping for joy to be out of that dangerous wood. In the afternoon, however, they found themselves at a rushing river that cut the road in two. On the other side, they could see the yellow brick road continuing across a beautiful landscape with green meadows dotted with colorful flowers.

"How are we going to get to that enchanting place?" asked Dorothy.

"It's easy!" answered the Scarecrow. "The Tin Woodman will build a raft with the trunks of the trees and we will use that to cross the river." So the Tin Woodman set to work again with his ax.

When night came, the raft was still not ready, so the group looked for a safe resting place for the Lion, Toto and Dorothy, who dreamt of the Emerald City and the great Oz, who would soon send her back home. The next morning our group of travelers started out enthusiastically. The big, dark forest with all its dangers was behind them, and in front of them lay a pleasant walk in the midst of wildflower meadows, as soon as they had crossed the river.

The raft was ready and Dorothy sat down in the middle of it with Toto next to her. When the Lion jumped aboard, the raft tilted dangerously, but luckily it did not tip over, and the Scarecrow and the Tin Woodman began to propel it forward using two long poles. For a few minutes, they moved without any difficulty in the direction of the opposite bank, but in the middle of the river, the water became so deep that the poles no longer touched the bottom.

"Oh, no! This is not good!" exclaimed the Tin Woodman. "If we can't steer the raft we risk ending up in the land of the Witch of the West, and I will never get my heart."

"Nor I my brain," cried the Scarecrow. "We simply must get to the Emerald City." And so saying, he pushed the pole with such force that it stuck into the bottom of the river and before he could let it go the current dragged the raft away, leaving him hanging from the pole, in the middle of the river.

"Goodbye, my friends," he called out to his companions as they drifted away.

The Tin Woodman began to cry, but he remembered in time that the tears would rust him and he tried to stop, even if everyone was deeply sad about the fate of the Scarecrow, who, in the meantime, was thinking, "This is definitely not an improvement. Before, I was hanging from a pole in my back, but I was standing in the middle of a cornfield, where I could at least talk to the crows, while a scarecrow in the middle of a river is completely useless!"

The raft continued to drift away along the river, carried by the current. "We must do something!" exclaimed the Lion after a few minutes. "I can swim to the shore, pulling the raft behind me, if you will hold my tail tightly in your hands." As soon as he said this, he took a deep breath and jumped into the water, and the Tin Woodman seized his tail. It was an enormous effort, but eventually the Lion managed to drag the raft to the shore. Exhausted, the friends sat for some minutes wondering what was the best thing to do. "We have to go back and help the Scarecrow and then find the yellow brick road again," Dorothy decided finally. So they walked along the bank of the river, in search of the friend from whom they had been separated by the current. They found him just as they had left him, perched on his pole in the middle of the river, with a sad expression on his face. They were sitting sat on the bank trying to think of a way to save him when a stork flew over their heads. "Who are you? And where are you going?" asked the bird.

"We're going to the Emerald City," said Dorothy.

"This is not the way. Are you lost?"

"No. We know we have to get back to the yellow brick road, but we first have to save our friend, the Scarecrow, who's down there."

"I'll see to it!" replied the stork, then took off and glided down to the Scarecrow. He grabbed him with his strong legs and carried him to the shore, where his traveling companions embraced him, laughing. "Thank you stork!" they called out to the bird. who was now flying away.

In the best of moods, the travelers resumed their journey, and found themselves crossing a large field of poppies. "Look, how beautiful!" cried Dorothy, breathing the sweet scent of the flowers. However, it is well known that the scent of poppies is so powerful that anyone who breathes it is likely to fall asleep and never wake up, unless he is immediately taken away from the flowers. But Dorothy did not know that, and she continued walking, stopping to smell the larger flowers, until her eyelids became strangely heavy and she could not help but stop and close her eyes.

But the Tin Woodman knew what danger the little girl was in and decided to intervene. "We have to get out of this poppy field right away! Scarecrow, help me." And, holding Dorothy up, they carried on walking until the child could no longer stand up and she fell asleep. "What will we do?" asked the Lion. "If we leave her here, she will die! In fact, I think the fragrance of these flowers will kill us all, I can feel my eyes are closing and Toto is already asleep." But the Tin Woodman and the Scarecrow, being made of tin and straw, did not feel the strange effects of the perfume.

"Lion, this is what we'll do: you run as fast as you can. You are so heavy that we would never be able to carry you out of this field," declared the Scarecrow. "In the meantime we'll try to save Dorothy and Toto, but don't you fall asleep because if you do, I don't know what we could to help you!" The Lion leapt ahead and with three great bounds disappeared from view. The Tin Woodman and the Scarecrow crossed their hands and made a seat with which to carry Dorothy and Toto across the poppy field. They walked and walked, and it seemed that the poppies would never end. Passing a bend in a river, they saw the Lion lying on the ground, sound asleep just where the flowers gave way to fields of grass.

"No! Poor friend!" exclaimed the Tin Woodman. "We can't do anything for him," said the Scarecrow. "We must leave him here to sleep forever." "Maybe he will dream of being the bravest of the animals. Come on now, we need to carry Dorothy away from these flowers or she will suffer the same fate."

Passing the last of the poppies, the little girl stretched and started to stir. They set her down on the soft grass, with Toto next to her and waited for the fresh air to blow away the last of poisonous scent. "We are almost at the place where the current dragged us away," remarked the Scarecrow. "We must be near the yellow brick road, don't you think?"

The Tin Woodman was about to reply when he heard a loud roar: turning round he saw a strange animal, like an enormous tabby cat, busy chasing a field mouse. Although he had no heart, the Tin Woodman felt that he could not allow the big cat to kill this helpless little creature, so he raised his ax threateningly and frightened the beast so much that it turned and ran away whimpering.

The little mouse approached the group of friends and said, in a squeaky little voice: "Thank you! You saved my life."

"But of course!" the Tin Woodman answered proudly. "Even if I do not have a heart, I try to help anyone in need, even a simple little animal."

"A simple little animal? I am the Queen of the field mice," cried the little mouse, indignantly.

"Oh, it's a pleasure to meet Your Majesty," replied the Scarecrow with a deep bow. At that moment, hundreds of mice appeared. Seeing their Queen safe and sound they began to speak with one voice: "Your Majesty, what a relief! We thought you lost! How did you escape the tabby cat?" "It was this tin man who helped me. He and his friends deserve our gratitude. We are at their service!" said the Queen. "Is there anything we can do for you?"

And the Scarecrow, who had been thinking about the Lion sleeping *a few steps away from them, said, "There is one thing. Can you help us save our friend the Lion, who is sleeping in the poppy field?"*

"A lion?" cried the Queen. "It's too dangerous! He'll eat us all!"

"No, he's a coward; he'll do you no harm."

"What a curious thing: a cowardly lion. We trust you, but what can we do?"

"Gather all your people together, and have every mouse bring with him a piece of string. Meanwhile, my friend the Tin Woodman will build a cart to transport the Lion: we will hoist him up and you mice can pull it as far as here."

So that is what they did, and just as thousands of mice flocked to the call of their Queen, Dorothy awoke and was astonished by the scene unfolding before her eyes. The Tin Woodman and the Scarecrow hugged her happily, then presented her to the Queen and explained their plan to help their friend. All the mice had attached their pieces of string to the cart and the whole party went back to the place where the Lion lay asleep. With great difficulty, the big animal was hoisted onto the wagon and pulled by the mice to where Dorothy was waiting anxiously. The mice were then detached from the cart and, having said their farewells, scattered among the grass along with the Queen. Dorothy and her friends then sat down beside the Lion, waiting for him to wake up.

When at last he awoke, the Lion was very happy to see them all:

"I was so scared!" he exclaimed. "I ran as fast as I could, but then I fell asleep. How did you save me?" They told him about the field mice and the Lion laughed, "And me always trying to look big and scary! Then I almost get myself killed by little flowers and rescued by tiny country mice! I'm fine now. I can walk again. What will we do now?" he asked finally.

"We take the yellow brick road to Oz," Dorothy said firmly.

The group were soon on their way, and in no time at all they found the road to the Emerald City. Once again, the road was wide and lined with fences, all painted bright green. Dorothy noticed that even the farmers working in the fields were dressed in green, and their houses were green as well. "We must be getting close to the Emerald City," said the girl, and she went up timidly to one of the little green men who was working in a nearby field and asked, "Excuse me, we are on our way to the Emerald City to meet the Great Oz. Could you tell us how far we have to go?"

The little man looked astonished at this strange group and then replied, "You're almost there. But are you sure that the powerful Oz will see you? You know, no-one is allowed to meet him. He sits day after day in the great Throne Room, but he does not see anyone and not even his servants see him."

"That's very strange," replied Dorothy worriedly, "but we must see him. If not, I will not be able to go home and the Lion will not have *any courage. The Scarecrow needs a brain and the Tin Woodman will never be happy without a heart!"*

"I can see that your reasons are serious and important! I truly hope that Oz wants to help you! Good luck!"

Dorothy bade farewell to the kind little man and the party continued on their way. The green farmer was not wrong, for after little more than an hour,

THEY SAW IN THE SKY AHEAD OF THEM A MAGNIFICENT GREEN GLOW: THEY HAD ARRIVED AT THE EMERALD CITY!

Before them rose a great, green wall studded with emeralds, which made it sparkle so much that it dazzled even the Scarecrow's painted eyes. The group went up to the great gate next to which they found a little man dressed from head to foot in green who asked them, "What brings you to the Emerald City?" "We are here to see the Great Oz," replied Dorothy. The little man was astonished to hear these words. "I have been on guard at the city gate for years and no-one has ever asked to see the powerful Wizard of Oz! I... look, I am not sure it's possible. You could make him very angry if you interrupted his wise and mysterious reflections with foolish requests."

"But our requests are not foolish, they are very important!" exclaimed Dorothy. "And we were told that Oz is a good wizard."

"Indeed he is. He rules wisely. And since you asked me to lead you

to him, I have no choice. I will take you to the palace. But first you must put on these spectacles," he said, picking up a large box from which he pulled a pair of enormous and comical spectacles for everyone, even for Toto.

"Why do we have to wear them?" asked the astonished Lion.

"Because otherwise the bright light of the Emerald City would blind you. All the inhabitants of the city must wear them day and night: this is what Oz ordered when the city was built," replied the Guardian of the Gate, locking with a little lock the spectacles that he had just put on Dorothy, so that she could not take them off. This done, he opened the gate and they all followed him through the streets of the city.

If they had not been wearing the protective spectacles, Dorothy and her friends would have been blinded by the brightness of this splendid city. The houses that lined the street were adorned with emeralds, the windows were green, and so were the streets and the clothes of the people who thronged the streets, and who turned to look in surprise at

33

the strange group that was following the Guardian.

At last, they arrived at the palace, which shone more brightly than any other building. A guard accompanied them as far as the entrance to the Throne Room and then said, "Wait for me here. I will announce your arrival to the Great Oz." When the guard came back out of the Throne Room, they ran to meet him. "Did you see Oz?" asked Dorothy. "Certainly not! I've never seen him, but I spoke to him and at first he was angry. Then he asked me what you look like, and when I told him about your red boots, he decided that he would receive you. You first, little girl: follow me." And without waiting for a reply he turned to open the door. Dorothy went in behind him, and, somewhat afraid, entered the Throne Room, speechless.

She had come into a large circular room, with a high ceiling from which poured a brilliant light like that of the sun, which made the emeralds embedded in the walls shine. But what surprised Dorothy more than anything was the enormous Head that she saw placed on top of the throne. It had no hair, no arms, no legs or any other part of the body, but eyes, a nose, and a mouth, and it was as big as the head of a giant. While Dorothy was still looking at it in astonishment, the Head spoke: "I am Oz, the Great and Terrible. Who are you and why do you seek me? And above all where did you get those red boots?"

"My name is Dorothy, I come from Kansas and I have come to ask for your help. I would like you to send me back home. The boots aren't mine. I got them from the Wicked Witch of the East when my cabin fell on her and flattened her," explained Dorothy in a whisper. The great Head observed her for a moment, and then said, "In my country, everyone must pay for what he gets. If you want me to send you back to Kansas, to use my extraordinary magical power for such an unusual thing, you must first do something for me. You help me and I will help you. Kill the Wicked Witch of the West!"

"But I can't," cried Dorothy, puzzled. "Of course you can. You killed the Wicked Witch of the East! Do what I ask of you and I will help you." Hearing these words, Dorothy began to weep with disappointment. She had never hurt anyone in her whole life. How could she kill a witch who was so evil that not even Oz had been able to defeat her?

"That is my last word," added Oz. "Now you can go and confer with your friends. I will not receive them or hear their requests as long as the Wicked Witch of the West is alive."

Discouraged, the girl left the Throne Room and went to tell her friends all that Oz had said. "There is no hope," she concluded at the end of her story.

"What's to be done?" she asked.

"There's only one thing to do in my opinion. Find the Wicked Witch of the West and destroy her. Otherwise I will never have the courage that I desire," said the Lion.

"And I will never have a heart," added the Tin Woodman.

*"AND I THE BRAIN THAT I WANT MORE THAN ANY-
THING," CONCLUDED THE SCARECROW.*

*Now Dorothy stopped weeping and whispered, "Alright, let's try.
Although I'm sure I don't want to kill anyone, even if it is the only
way back to Aunt Em."*

*So it was decided that they would leave the following day, and at
dawn they left the Emerald City and started walking toward the
kingdom of the Wicked Witch of the West. You need to know that
this witch had only one eye, but the eye that she had was so powerful that she could see great distances, and so she was able to see
Dorothy, the Lion, the Scarecrow and the Tin Woodman coming toward her castle. They were still a very long way away, but they had
already crossed the border that marked the beginning of her territory,
and this made her angry.*

*She took out a silver whistle that hung around her neck, and blew
it. Immediately, she was surrounded by a great flock of crows, led
by their Queen, and the Witch gave them this order: "I want you to
tear those strangers apart! Fly at them, peck their eyes out, do as you
want, but stop them!"*

*The flock rose into the air and flew in the direction of the friends.
Seeing them coming, the Scarecrow went ahead confidently and ex-*

claimed, "This is my fight. I'll take care of it. Don't worry. None of these crows will hurt you." So they lay down on the ground behind him, while the Scarecrow opened his arms and started to flap them. Seeing him, the crows became afraid, but their Queen encouraged them. "It's only a man stuffed with straw, why are you scared? Follow me!" she said, and swooped at the Scarecrow, but he quickly spun round and sent her flying against a tree and killed her. Another crow flew at him and the Scarecrow repeated the same deadly move. He did this forty times, killing all of them.

When the Witch saw what had happened, she was furious. She blew twice on her silver whistle, calling up a swarm of big, black bees. "Sting the strangers to death!" she ordered, and the bees flew with a great buzzing toward Dorothy and her friends, who were still walking toward the castle. The Lion was the first to see them coming, but the Scarecrow had another idea and said to the Tin Woodman, "Cover Dorothy, Toto and the Lion with straw from your stuffing so that the bees cannot sting them!" The Tin Woodman did as he was told, and so when the bees arrived they found only him waiting for them. They hurled themselves against him but they split their stingers. They could not hurt him and they all died. Dorothy and the Lion helped the Tin Woodman to stuff the straw back into the Scarecrow, and then the companions went on their way. Seeing her bees vanquished, the Wicked Witch was so angry that her teeth chattered and she tore her hair out. Then she grabbed her whistle once again and with three strong blasts called up a pack of giant wolves.

The Tin Woodman was the first to hear the beasts creeping toward them in the woods, and he exclaimed to his friends, "This is my fight! Stay behind me and let me face them." He took up the sharp ax and when the first wolf reached him, he swung it in the air and then brought it down on him. One by one all the wolves fell beneath his blows.

Seeing that not even her terrible wolves could stop the travelers, the Witch decided to resort to the Golden Cap. This was a magic cap with the power to call up the Winged Monkeys, who were obliged by a spell to obey her orders. But no-one may call on these creatures more than three times, and the Witch had already used the magic cap twice. She had only one chance left. In the end, she decided to do it. She put the Golden Cap on and recited the spell. Immediately she heard a low rumble and the rustling of a great many wings. Then out of the clouds came dozens of large Winged Monkeys. The largest of all came up to her and exclaimed, "You have called us for the third and last time. What is your command?"

"I want you to destroy those insolent brutes who dare to trespass on my land. All except the Lion. Bring him to me safe and sound. I want him to draw my carriage." The monkeys rose into the air and soon reached Dorothy and her companions. The first of them grabbed the

Scarecrow; they pulled out all his stuffing and threw it up into a tree. Others took hold of the Tin Woodman and lifted him up above a ravine. Then they dropped him into it, battering him so badly that he could not even speak any more. Next, they tied the Lion up ready to take him to the Witch's palace and finally they turned threateningly toward Dorothy. But when they saw the kiss of the Good Witch of the North on her forehead, they stopped, deciding to take the girl with them to the palace.

"We dare not harm this little girl. She is protected by the Power of Good. The Witch must take care of it!" declared the King of the Winged Monkeys, and they carried Dorothy and the Lion carefully to the castle. "We have obeyed you," he now said to the Witch, "never dare to call on us again!"

When she saw the Good Witch of the North's kiss shining on the girl's forehead, the Witch realized that not even she could do her any harm. But when she looked down and saw the red boots she started to tremble with fear, thinking that Dorothy was herself a sorceress endowed with great power. But the child's innocent and terrified look showed her that she did not know of the magical power of the boots, and so the Witch decided to steal them from her at the first opportunity. She locked the Lion in a large cage and sent Dorothy to the kitchens where she was to wash pots and sweep floors, while she worked out a plan to steal the magic boots.

In the end, the wicked creature came up with a trap. She stretched an invisible thread across the door to the kitchen, and when Dorothy passed by she tripped and fell, losing one of the red boots, which the Witch immediately grabbed and put on her own foot. "Give it back," cried Dorothy. "No, now it's mine," laughed the Witch, "and one of these days I will take the other from you too!" At these words, Dorothy became so angry that she took up a bucket of water and emptied it over the Witch's head. At once, the wicked old thing screamed in terror, and then she started to melt! Dorothy was astonished!

"Look what you've done," howled the Witch, "How did you find out that water, and only water, has the power to kill me?"

"I... I'm very sorry," stammered Dorothy, terrified at the sight of the Witch melting in front of her very eyes like sugar in water. And then, with a last shrill cry, the Witch turned into a dark shapeless mass on the flagstones.

Plucking up her courage, Dorothy hurried to clean the floor with more water. She put on the boot that the Witch had stolen and ran to free the Lion and give him the news:

THE WICKED WITCH OF THE WEST WAS DEAD!

The cowardly Lion roared with joy to hear it, and the two friends decided to tell the Winkies, who for years had been the wicked old woman's slaves. The Winkies were so happy that they arranged a

great festival for that same evening in Dorothy's honor. But the little girl was not so happy. She could not stop thinking about the Tin Woodman and the Scarecrow.

"If only we could rescue them," she sighed.

The little yellow men promised that they would try to help, and a group of them left straight away in search of their two companions. After two days traveling, they found the Tin Woodman at the bottom of the ravine, all battered and rusty. When Dorothy saw him, she could not help but cry, but one of the Winkies consoled her: "We have some very fine tinsmiths among us," he said. "They will certainly know how to help your friend!" When the tinsmiths arrived, they went straight to work to beat out the dents and oil the tin man's joints, and for three days and three nights, they were kept busy bending, polishing, and soldering, until the Tin Woodman was back in shape and finally able to move again. When Dorothy saw him, she hugged him tight and said, "If only the Scarecrow were with us!" So it was decided that the next day they would go to look for their friend, but when at last they came to the tree on which the Winged Monkeys had scattered his straw and his clothes, they saw that it was very tall. But the Tin Woodman was not discouraged. He took up his new ax and in no time at all, the tree was cut down, and the straw was scattered here and there.

The Winkies gathered it up and began patiently to stuff Scarecrow and sew his clothes back together, and at last his friends welcomed him back with smiles and tears of emotion.

Hearing the story of all that had happened, the Scarecrow exclaimed, "If the Witch is dead, we can return to the Emerald City and ask Oz to keep his promise!"

"Let's leave tomorrow morning! What do you think?" suggested Dorothy, and that is what they decided to do.

But the Winkies begged the Tin Woodman to stay and govern their land. The tin man was very tempted by the offer, and promised to return as soon as he had received his new heart from Oz.

Now the Winkies, resigned, loaded the friends with gifts, and gave to Dorothy, their savior, the most precious gift of all, the Golden Cap, explaining how to use it to summon the Winged Monkeys three times. Dorothy was very upset. "I'm not a witch, I don't know what to do with such powerful magic!" she exclaimed.

Once more, it was the Scarecrow who had a good idea. "We could use it to command the Winged Monkeys to carry us to the Emerald City!" he exclaimed. "We would be in Oz in a matter of a few hours." Dorothy agreed and recited the magic formula. Immediately the sun went in and the Winged Monkeys appeared from behind the clouds.

The King of the Monkeys bowed deeply and asked, "What is your command?"

"We want to go to the Emerald City."

"We will carry you! Climb up!" Dorothy and her friends hauled themselves onto the backs of the Winged Monkeys and they rose into the air. The girl could never have imagined that flying could be such fun and she was a little disappointed that the journey was so brief. In fact, after only a short time, the friends glimpsed the shimmering walls of the Emerald City.

After once again putting on the glasses that the Guardian of the Gate gave them, the four friends crossed the city to the Throne Room. When they entered the palace, the guard was speechless. This strange group had managed to kill the terrible Witch of the West? He must tell the Powerful Oz right away!

The guard disappeared into the Throne Room and returned hours later, asking the four travelers to go in all together.

They all expected to see Oz looking the same way as when he had appeared to Dorothy, so they were astonished to find the Throne Room empty and to hear only a deafening voice thunder,

"I AM OZ, THE GREAT AND TERRIBLE. WHY DO YOU SEEK ME?"

The four friends approached the empty throne and Dorothy said, "We are here to ask you to keep your promise! You said that if we destroyed the Witch of the West, you would grant our wishes!"

43

Wanting to confirm Dorothy's explanation, the Lion let out a roar so long and so mighty that little Toto ran away, terrified. As he ran, the little dog knocked over a screen in the corner of the room, and everyone was amazed to see hiding behind it a little old man, with a bald head and a wrinkled face.

"Who are you?" asked Dorothy. "I am... I am Oz, the... the Great and Terrible Oz," stammered the little old man. The four friends stared at him astounded. "I thought you were a great head!" whispered Dorothy. "What else have you lied about? Are you or are you not a wizard?" she cried. "Calm down, my dear! This is who I am... I am really just a fake, I admit it," the little man finished with a smile. "But I saw you! You were an enormous head! How did you do it?" demanded Dorothy. "It was just one of my tricks, a puppet made of papier-mâché, with strings for the eyes and the mouth. The lights and your fear made it work!" concluded the little old man.

"But who are you really?" asked the Scarecrow. So, Oz started to tell his story. "I was born close to your Kansas, little Dorothy. I grew up in a circus and one day I became a balloonist. I took to the air in a hot air balloon to attract spectators. One terrible day, though, the ropes that held the balloon down broke, and I flew up to the clouds where a strong wind caught me and brought me here. When I finally managed to get down, I was surrounded by the people of this region, who, seeing me come down from the skies, believed me to be great wizard. I let them think that, and accepted their invitation to govern them. I had the Emerald City built and, to justify its name, I ordered that everyone should put on green glasses." "But why? The city is not the color of emeralds?" asked Dorothy astonished. "No. It's a beautiful city, but it's the green lenses in the glasses that give it its green color. Another of my tricks, I'm afraid. Look, I think I'm a good man at heart, but I am really a rubbish wizard!" replied Oz.

"And the gifts that you promised?" cried the Tin Woodman. "Will I never have a heart?" Oz looked for a long time at Dorothy's friends, and then he replied, "Yes, Tin Woodman, I can give you what you asked me for, starting with your heart."

"I'm so excited!" said the Tin Woodman, while Oz fumbled about in a large trunk behind him.

"First," said the little man, "I have to cut a little hole in your tin chest. There! Now we hide this!" and so saying, he showed the Tin Woodman the elegant silk heart that he had taken out of the trunk. "It is a kind heart," he said, tying it tightly inside the Tin Woodman's chest and closing the square hole. "There, now! How do you feel?" "I cannot describe how much better I feel!" said the tin man, deeply moved.

"Now it's your turn, Scarecrow. Sit on that seat and let me look at that head of yours." And coming up to him, the little old man prodded and poked his head for a long time. Then, nodding to himself, he unstitched the top of the Scarecrow's head and slid in a handful of bran and some pins and needles, and mixed them in well with the straw before sewing it back up again. "How do you feel?" Dorothy asked the Scarecrow. "Very wise!" he replied, seriously. Now it was the Lion's turn. Oz climbed up onto an old cupboard, took down a golden bottle and poured half of the liquid it contained into a saucer. "This is essence of courage," he explained. "Drink it and your wish will be granted!" Without hesitating, the Lion drank all the liquid and licked his whiskers. It tasted good, this courage. It tasted of orangeade! "How do you feel now?" asked Oz. "Full of courage!" exclaimed the Lion, shaking his mane.

Oz looked at the three friends and congratulated each one of them, and smiled to himself to think how easy it was to convince them that they had received as a gift that which was already inside them. It would be somewhat more difficult to send Dorothy back home!

But at that moment, he had an idea. It was risky but it was certainly worth trying! Oz asked the girl to be patient and to wait three days. On the morning of the fourth day, when Dorothy had just about given up hope, he called her to him. When the little girl entered the Throne Room, Oz said to her, "My dear, I think I have found the way to get you out of this land," he said. "To return to Kansas?" asked Dorothy impatiently. "Well, of this I am not at all sure. There are many risks, but it's the only way. This is what I was thinking. I arrived here aboard a hot air balloon, you in the midst of a tornado, so I'm sure that the sky is the way we must go! Come with me and I will show you what I have been building!" Saying this, he took Dorothy by the hand and led her to the palace gardens.

"A HOT AIR BALLOON?" SAID DOROTHY, POINTING TO THE GREAT, GREEN, SILK BALLOON LYING AMONG THE FLOWERS.

"I don't know how to fly a hot air balloon!" she said, frightened. "But I do!" replied Oz with a wink. "Are you saying that you are coming with me? You?"

"Yes! I'm tired of being an impostor, and of being shut in the palace so as not to reveal to my subjects that I am not really the powerful magician they think I am! I would really like to return to Kansas and go back to work in the circus. And so tomorrow, Oz the Powerful will bid farewell to his people and we'll be off."

The next morning all the inhabitants of the Emerald City gathered at the hot air balloon to witness the extraordinary spectacle. Dorothy had said goodbye to her friends, hugging them and weeping for a long time, while Oz inflated the balloon. When he had finished he turned to the people and said, "I am going to visit my brother who lives among the clouds. While I am away, the Scarecrow will rule in my place. He is wise and good and I order you to obey him as you have obeyed me." Oz was still speaking when a great wind suddenly blew up. "Come, Dorothy," cried the little old man, but the little girl did not make it in time... Crac!

The cables that held the balloon broke, and it rose into the air without her.

"Come back!" cried Dorothy. "I need to get on! I have to come with you!"

"I can't come back my dear, I'm sorry! Farewell!" cried Oz as the balloon rose high into the sky.

Soon the green balloon disappeared behind a cloud, and that was the last she saw of the Great and Powerful Wizard of Oz. For all we know he might have returned home safe and sound and perhaps at this very moment he is enchanting the circus audience with his ventriloquist act.

Everyone stared for a long time at the cloud behind which he had disappeared, singing his praises with affection: "He was always good to us," they said. "And he left the wise Scarecrow to govern us." But Dorothy could not stop weeping, seeing that her hopes of returning home had been dashed. She was so sad that the Tin Woodman was deeply moved, and risked becoming rusty with his tears. The Scarecrow became sad too, and he invited the friends to join him in the Throne Room to try to console Dorothy and to talk about everything that had happened that day.

"When I think that only a few days ago I was hanging from a pole in the middle of a field and now I am master of this splendid city and this beautiful palace, I simply cannot believe our luck!" exclaimed the Scarecrow from the Throne on which he sat.

"We can live here happily together if Dorothy wanted to stay in the Emerald City," he added. "But I don't want to stay here!" bawled the little girl, holding Toto tight in her arms. "I want to go back to Aunt Em and Uncle Henry!"

"What can we do to help her?" asked the Lion.

The Scarecrow started to think over the question and thought so long and so hard that his pins started to make holes in his fabric. "Why not call the Winged Monkeys?" he suggested at last.

Dorothy perked up when she heard these words: "A brilliant idea! Scarecrow, your new brain is working perfectly," and, smiling for the first time in hours, Dorothy put on the Golden Cap and called the King of the Monkeys, who at once came in the window and stood before her.

"This is the second time that you have called on us," said the King. "What is your command?"

"*I WANT TO RETURN HOME TO MY AUNT AND UNCLE. CAN YOU HELP ME CROSS THE GREAT DESERT?*"

The King of the Monkeys shook his head. "I'm sorry but I can't do that. We belong to this land. We can't leave."

"So there is no-one who can help me," said Dorothy, drying the tears that were running down her cheeks once more.

"Perhaps Glinda can help you," replied the King of the Monkeys.

"Who is Glinda?" asked the Tin Woodman.

"She is the Witch of the South, the most powerful of all four of the witches who ruled the lands around the Emerald City. She rules over the Quadlings, and her palace lies right on the edge of the desert. But getting there is not easy. The road to the south is full of dangers, wild beasts, and strange creatures. Good luck," concluded the Winged Monkey before flying away through the window.

"I will go south with Dorothy. After all, I owe my courage to her," said the Lion.

"It's true," agreed the Tin Woodman. "Without her I would still be rusted stiff in the woods. I'm coming with you too."

"We'll all go," said the Scarecrow.

"Thank you, my friends," whispered Dorothy gratefully. Then she stopped weeping, got up and smoothed her skirt, saying, "Let's leave right away!"

Soon the little group was once more on the road and came to the city gate where the Guardian took off their green glasses and wished them good luck on their journey, saying to the Scarecrow, "You'll come back soon, won't you? Now you are our ruler and we need your wisdom."

"I will be back as soon as Dorothy has found her way home," the Scarecrow reassured him.

The four friends headed south, laughing and chatting.

The sun was shining and Dorothy felt renewed hope that she would be able to return to her aunt and uncle. The Tin Woodman and the Scarecrow were happy to be able to help, and the Lion and Toto were happy to be able to run free in the wildflower meadows.

They kept on walking until they reached a dense forest, where they came to a halt, as they looked for a way through the trees.

The Scarecrow walked up to a large oak tree, but as soon as he bent to pass under its branches, they reached down and twined around his body, lifted him up, and threw him into the meadow. The Scarecrow was well padded, and he was not hurt, but when the branches grabbed Toto, the dog began to yelp in pain.

THE TIN WOODMAN WENT UP TO IT
AND SWUNG HIS AX
WITH A BLOW SO STRONG THAT

Immediately the tree raised all its branches and began to shake them as if crying in rage and pain. The four friends rushed under the tree and passed by unscathed.

Dorothy made sure that Toto was not hurt and then, holding him tightly in her arms, she joined her friends, who were making their way through the forest, where no more trees tried to attack them.

"But what happened? Why did that big oak try to stop us?" asked the little girl, who was still afraid.

"I think it was a guardian of the forest," explained the Tin Woodman.

"It is a tree with special powers whose task is to keep out strangers."

Mulling over their strange adventure, the four friends reached the edge of the woods and there they saw something that surprised them very much.

A high wall, which seemed to be made of white china, barred their way.

"And now what will we do?" asked Dorothy.

"We need a ladder," said the Tin Woodman, and he started to cut branches and twigs. In the meantime, his friends continued to examine the great wall.

"I really don't understand what it is made of," said the Scarecrow, after thinking hard for a long time.

"Rest your new brain, my friend," answered the Tin Woodman, "and don't worry about the wall. This ladder will help us to get over it, and see what's on the other side." Saying this, the Tin Woodman picked up the ladder he had made, and which was actually a bit rickety, but tall enough to allow everyone to get to the top of the wall. What the friends saw from the top took their breath away. "Oh, my!" cried the Scarecrow, peering over the top. Then he climbed further and perched himself on top of the wall.

"Oh, my!" repeated Dorothy when she joined him. When all the friends had climbed up, they exclaimed over the strange landscape that lay before their eyes: vast fields, white and smooth as a china tray, were dotted with houses made entirely of china and painted in bright colors. Even the animals seemed to be made of the same material. But most surprising of all were the small inhabitants of this strange country. There were princesses in colorful clothes, dancers wearing fluffy tutus, princes wearing crowns studded with gemstones, and clowns with cone-shaped hats. Dorothy even saw a dog just like Toto and he, like everyone else, was made entirely of china. The friends jumped down from the wall and the little dog came up to Toto, but as soon as Toto gave him a little push with his nose to ask him to play, the little ceramic dog fell down and broke his tail.

"Look what you've done!" shouted a shepherdess. "You've broken my dog's tail! Now I have to take him to the mender's to have him glue it back on."

"I'm very sorry," said Dorothy, holding on tightly to Toto to stop him making any more trouble. "We have to be very careful," said the Tin Woodman, "or we will hurt these fragile and delicate creatures."

A little further on, the Lion almost collided with a finely dressed princess.

"Look out!" cried the pretty little statue, "I most certainly do not want a crack in my beautiful face."

"You really are very beautiful," said Dorothy. "Would you like to come back to Kansas with me? You could you live on Aunt Em's mantelpiece. If you want, you can climb into my basket and..."

"Absolutely not! It would make me very unhappy!" the princess exclaimed indignantly. "You need to know that here in our land we live very contented lives, and we can walk around and talk as we wish. But if we go beyond the borders of this land, we become stiff and cold, and we can only stand still. Of course, those who put us on their shelves or tables like that, but we don't!"

"I would never want to make you unhappy!" exclaimed the girl, surprised. "I'd rather say goodbye. And I assure you that we'll all leave right away so that we don't do any more damage."

The travelers resumed their journey, proceeding with great caution through the china country. As they passed, people and animals moved away from them to avoid being broken, and after a few hours of walking, the group reached the other wall that marked the border of the kingdom. It was lower than the first, and they managed to get over it by climbing on the back of the lion, who then joined them with a great leap. "Today I found out that there is something worse than being made of rags and straw. It must be terrible to be broken so easily," remarked the Scarecrow, as they walked away from that strange country.

After walking all day, Dorothy, who was very tired, asked her friends to stop and rest. It was now dark, and it was impossible to tell where they had camped until morning, when they realized they were at the edge of a large forest of ancient trees, the tallest they had ever seen. "What a lovely place!" said the Lion, looking around with eyes sparkling with joy. "I would love to live here, I wonder if there are any other beasts?" And, as if in answer to the Lion's question, they heard coming from the depths of the forest a noise that sounded like many animals at the same time. When they reached a clearing in the middle of the forest, they realized what was making the noise: "It's a meeting of animals," cried the Lion, pointing to hundreds of animals of all species.

Tigers, bears, foxes, wolves, and other species that Dorothy did not recognize, were engaged in a heated discussion over a question that seemed to worry them greatly.

When they saw the Lion with his friends, the animals fell silent and a tigress came forward and said, "Welcome, King of Beasts! You have arrived just in time to help us defeat our enemy and restore peace in the forest."

"What's wrong?" asked the Lion.

"A while ago, a terrible monster came to terrorize us. It wanders the woods in search of us animals, to catch us and eat us. It's like a big spider, and it's as big as an elephant. We have called this meeting to decide what to do, but then you came along. Please, help us! Defeat the monster and become our king."

"With pleasure!" exclaimed the Lion, and with a roar he leapt away to look for the creature. He found it not far away, asleep under a tree. It looked so hideous and frightening that the Lion was happy to have received his courage, otherwise he would have run away as fast as he could.

After watching the huge spider for a long time, the Lion realized that to defeat him he must surprise him in his sleep. Without wasting any more time, the Lion leapt on the monster and knocked its head off with his great

paw, then went back to the clearing and announced: "The monster has been defeated! There's no need to be afraid anymore!"

Hearing those words, all the animals bowed deeply, then howled, growled, grunted, and then cheered the Lion, their King. The Lion promised them that he would return to rule them as soon as Dorothy was able to leave for Kansas, and then resumed his journey with his friends.

Coming out of the forest, the little band was faced with a steep and high hill, covered with big rocks. "Come, my friends, it will be a tiring climb but we have no alternative," said the Scarecrow, starting to climb over the boulders.

But he had gone only a short way when he heard a voice shouting, "Stop there! You are not allowed to climb our hill!"

"Who said that?" In answer to the Scarecrow, a strange creature appeared from behind a rock. It was as tall as a column, with a large rectangular head, but no arms. When the Scarecrow saw that he had no arms, he thought that this strange man would not be able to stop him, and he ran up the slope. Quick as lightning, the man's head shot forward and his neck stretched out of all proportion, until it struck the Scarecrow, who rolled down the hill. Straight away, the man's neck went back into his body and his head returned to its place, then the Hammer-Head was joined by hundreds of others of his kind who began to spin their heads most threateningly. "It's pointless to keep

fighting with these people, no-one can survive a blow from their hammer-heads," said the Tin Woodman, helping the Scarecrow to his feet.

"What can we do, then?" asked the Lion.

"Dorothy, call the Winged Monkeys," suggested the Scarecrow after a few moments of reflection. "They must help you a third and final time."

"Good idea! I'll do it right away," said Dorothy, who was already wearing the Golden Cap.

A few moments after uttering the magic formula, the girl saw the Monkey King appear from behind the clouds and he landed next to her. "What is your command?" he asked. "Carry us over this hill to the castle of the Witch of the South." The Winged Monkeys picked up the four friends and flew with them over the hill, while the Hammer-Heads stretched their necks in vain, trying to hit them. In a short time, the monkeys carried Dorothy and her friends safe and sound to the entrance of the castle of Glinda, the Good Witch of the South. "This was the last of the three commands that you may give me. Goodbye and good luck," said the King of the Monkeys, rising into the air. Dorothy waved goodbye and then followed her friends inside Glinda's castle.

The Good Witch of the South was waiting for them in the Throne Room.

She was beautiful, with long red hair and gentle blue eyes. As soon as her eyes fell on Dorothy, she smiled sweetly and asked, "How can I help you, my child?" The girl told her story, explaining how she had arrived in this world, how she had met her friends, the adventures they had had, and how much she wanted to go home. "It's my dearest wish! By now Aunt Em must be convinced that something terrible has happened to me. Can you help me?" she asked the Witch hopefully. Glinda leaned towards her to kiss her forehead and said, "I think I can help you, but in return I would like the Golden Cap."

"Of course! I no longer need it. Take it, it's yours," cried Dorothy.

"If you put it on you can call on the Winged Monkeys three times."

"And I think that I'll need their help," replied Glinda, smiling.

"Scarecrow," she added, "What are you going to do when Dorothy has gone back?"

"I would like to go back to the Emerald City. Oz asked me to govern it, and its inhabitants are loyal to me," replied the Scarecrow.

"So the first thing that I will ask of the Winged Monkeys is to guide you to the gates of the Emerald City, because its inhabitants deserve a ruler as wise as you are."

Having said that, Glinda turned to the Tin Woodman and asked, "What will you do when Dorothy returns home?"

The tin man thought for a moment and eventually said, "After the death of the Wicked Witch of the West, the Winkies were very nice

to me and asked me to rule them. I like their land and I think that the best thing for me would be to go back there!"

"My second command to the Winged Monkeys, then, will be to carry you as far as the land of the Winkies. Your kindness and your big heart will compensate them for their many years of slavery."

Finally, it was the turn of the Lion. The Witch of the South asked gently, "And you, my brave friend, what will you do after Dorothy has gone?"

"A few days ago we went through a great forest and all the animals that live there crowned me their King. I would be very happy to rule them and stay with them in that beautiful forest," cried the Lion, smiling.

"Then I will command the Winged Monkeys to take you back to the forest. It will be my third and final command, and then I will give the Golden cap to the King of the Monkeys, releasing him and his people from the curse that forces them to obey."

The Tin Woodman, the Scarecrow and the Lion thanked her for her kindness from the bottom of their hearts, and then Dorothy said timidly, "You really are as good and kind as you are beautiful, but still you have not told me how I can get back to Kansas."

"THE RED BOOTS WILL TAKE YOU HOME. TAP THE HEELS TOGETHER

replied Glinda, who added, "If you had known what incredible power there was in the boots of the Wicked Witch of the East, you could have gone home as soon as you arrived in our world."

"But if you had, I'd still be hanging from that pole in the middle of the field and I would never have got my brain," cried the Scarecrow. "I would have been a coward forever," said the Lion, "And I would never got my heart and I'd still be in the forest, rusting and alone," concluded the Tin Woodman, who started to weep in a way that was dangerous for his joints. Hearing these words Dorothy was moved as well.

She hugged her friends tight and thanked Glinda the Good for her kindness. She took Toto in her arms, and tapped the heels of the red boots together three times, saying, "Take me home to Aunt Em and Uncle Henry!" Now the world around her disappeared, and the child found herself flying through the air with the wind howling in her ears.

Then everything stopped abruptly and Dorothy found herself sitting in a field. Nervously, she opened her eyes to see where she had landed, and then exclaimed with a laugh, "Toto, we're home!"